CW01066546

CHANGING LIGHT

by

James Irvine

The Laverock's Nest Press
Tranent

First published in 2014 by

The Laverock's Nest Press
17 Carlaverock Drive
Tranent
East Lothian
EH33 2EE
Scotland

www.laverocks-nest-press.com

ISBN: 978 0 9928005 0 5

British Library Cataloguing in Publication Data. A catalogue record
for this book is available from the British Library.

Dedicated to my parents

With thanks to
Susan Boyd & Mary Scott
for their editorial assistance

CHANGING LIGHT

One

The Community of Kirknane* - circa 1980.

Stephen Whyte sat at his bedroom window and its view of the countryside that started right outside his flat. He would often sit there when thinking about things, from time to time looking out at the neighbouring fields and the hills beyond. This morning he was sitting there whilst waiting to leave at the right time for his meeting with Davina Corrie. He had little in the way of positive expectations for the meeting and was anticipating it being one more trial in his life so far in Kirknane: a life that effectively kept him a prisoner in his home.

Despite being born to parents who conformed to the social ethos of Kirknane, Stephen had always been 'different'. It seemed so to his parents almost since his birth. Anyone else he encountered more than simply in passing also became aware of his difference sooner or later. No-one, however, was more aware of his difference than he was himself.

Stephen had been a solitary child who was looked on by adults and other children alike as being unnaturally solemn, sensitive and withdrawn. Throughout his childhood he had no real friends. At school, he worked diligently and did reasonably well, but he developed a deep disdain for an education system that seemed innately hostile to his sensibility. This disdain, and his social austereness, alienated both his teachers and his fellow scholars, for they took it as haughty self-importance and condescending rejection. His childhood, both at home and at school, made him a very self-contained person, but his natural sensitivity continued to make him vulnerable to some extent.

After finishing his schooling, Stephen did not go on to higher education, as it seemed to promise a continuation of his unhappy experience of school. He also rejected a career for the sake of not inhibiting his true vocation, as he had for some time had a sense of an unrealised one, and thought a career would not only divert him from his true vocation once he found it, but might hinder it being found in the first place. Moreover, following a career in Kirknane involved extensive social participation not only within the workplace but outside it as well, and this was reason enough to him for not pursuing one. Instead, he took jobs that minimised the need

*kirk = church, nane = none

3

for social interaction, and where he could work on his own as much as possible, though he invariably found such jobs mundane and unsatisfying.

Stephen found the adult society of Kirknane no better than that of its children, and in many ways an extension of it. It was equally uninviting to participate in and incompatible with his nature and sensibility. It was a society he saw as pervasively coarse, superficial and materialistic. It valued togetherness over aloneness and eventful activity over passivity, but Stephen preferred his own company and quiet contemplation. In Kirknane, such preferences were considered anti-social and strange. As in his childhood, Stephen's general aloneness was looked on negatively, for it suggested someone unable or unwilling to participate properly in the life of the community and a rejection of its egalitarian and gregarious social ethos.

Through the common mundanities of daily life, his vigilance in public and his general reclusion in the shadows of community life, Stephen learned to obscure much of his difference from everyone else, but he was always aware of it to some degree, and sometimes grievously so. He came to see that the community had a power that everyone else seemed to enjoy and understand whereas to him that power seemed like a kind of covert enemy.

Outside of work, Stephen's main interests reflected his passive and solitary nature. In particular, he read a lot of the older literature that went unpublished and otherwise unread in Kirknane - in its original form at least - for it was regarded as difficult to read, involving unattractive characters, and boring and outdated in subject matter – and the older it was, the more outdated it was seen to be. A little of the older literature, considered more accessible and in some way relevant, was still published, but only then in simpler and abridged versions tailored for the contemporary reader, and they were now identified and treated as the originals. These books were themselves increasingly becoming replaced by film versions, and these films increasingly becoming identified and regarded as the original work. Stephen's copies of the older literature were the genuine originals that had been handed down through generations of his family. They retained everything that required an intelligent reading and that had thus been edited out of the simplified editions for contemporary readers. They had themselves become increasingly unread by Stephen's forebears, but a curiously abiding family sense of respect and propriety kept the books in the family's possession. Stephen found this small library a world he could escape to from the unpleasantness of Kirknane, for it was a world far more suited to his sensibility. He took great delight in the descriptiveness of the now archaic vocabulary of the older literature, and the sophisticated construction of its writing, though he sometimes let slip such archaic words in public to the general disapproval of others, spoken or unspoken, of its esotericism. When these moments took place, however, he sensed a vulnerability and saw a fear in the eyes of those showing disapproval as if they were being shown something they didn't want to see. In such reaction he could sense a power in those words and thus a power in the older literature also. Contemporary literature essentially celebrated and endorsed the community life that he disdained, so he usually avoided it. There was, in any case, very little of it, for watching films and television had largely replaced reading. What Stephen saw as the general cultural decline of Kirknane was made even worse for him due to its historical and continuing position of being a significant, highly productive cultural centre - nowadays centred on film - disproportionate to its size.

Although Stephen valued his solitude, his isolation and the lack of friends and of any family after his parents died made him more alone than he wished. If he could find a like spirit he would happily make them a friend. If he could find a woman he was attracted to, and who did not share the coarse attributes common to both the women and men of Kirknane, he would happily form a relationship with her. He had yet to meet such people, however, and he did not expect to, for he believed they did not exist. Even when he considered the possibility that they did exist, he thought his reclusion - and theirs - would make it extremely unlikely they would find each other. Nevertheless, at times he would attempt to develop social relationships with others. His awkward efforts, though, invariably failed when his essential difference could no longer be disguised or repressed.

Two

As Stephen walked to Davina Corrie's office, he was mindful, as usual, of his difference from others whenever he exchanged glances with the people he encountered on the way. He was mindful of it always, to some degree, and now he was on his way to a meeting he expected would extinguish any hope he had of resolving, and releasing him from, that difference. He saw the meeting as a part – perhaps the final part - of a process that had started one day two years ago when he discovered why he was different, and had sensed a real hope of resolving his difference.

Stephen could still vividly remember what happened that day. He was sitting at his bedroom window, doodling absent-mindedly in a jotter. Next to his bed, the radio was playing quietly. A song came on the radio that caught his attention. Beguiled by its pleasing melody and fine sentiment, he stopped doodling and listened more intently. As he listened, however, he was disappointed with the song's lyric. It was banal and cliché-ridden, and spoiling the song. He wondered what a better choice of words would be. A couple of lines came into his head and he wrote them down on the open pages of the jotter. Then he realised what he had done: he had written something! Something pretty good!

This joyous realisation triggered an effusion of inspiration from Stephen. In an ecstasy, all kinds of writing and ideas for writing poured forth. Not wanting to forget anything, he wrote it all down as it came to him, on any blank space he could find in the jotter. He did not pause to contemplate what he had written for fear of ending the flow prematurely. Eventually his inspiration dried up, but at what felt to him to be its natural conclusion. With it all safely gathered in his jotter, he basked in the satisfaction of what had happened and what he had become. He was now a writer!

Despite the surprise, Stephen's newly discovered vocation seemed very befitting to him and gave him a strong sense of purpose, and now that he had finally realised his vocation as a writer he felt fully vindicated in the course he had taken to allow for that vocation to emerge and be developed. What he had been encouraged to see as defects in himself and his way of life in Kirknane now became virtues necessary for his vocation: his detachment and seriousness for the proper attitude in his observation of the subject matter of his writing, his acute sensitivity to maximise his observation, his thoughtfulness to contemplate and evaluate his observation as fully as possible, his liking for the archaic but expressive vocabulary of the older literature and its sophisticated writing style for the best articulation of his observation, and his self-containment to make public his observation without fear of disfavour.

After the elation of his becoming a writer had subsided, Stephen carefully read over everything he had scribbled down in the jotter. He soon realised there was little of substance in what he had written but, motivated by his new found sense of vocation and encouraged by the quality of a few fragments, he resolved to build on what was there.

As Stephen developed his writing, Kirknane provided its subject matter. In this way, his writing became a means of engaging with and relating to Kirknane as a community in a manner and to an extent he had never experienced before. It also gave Stephen a sense of power, essentially an enhancement of the power from the older literature, in opposition to the power of the community he struggled against. This made him wonder if he was inherently a writer from birth and this condition had led to his situation in Kirknane, or that his situation in Kirknane had made him become a writer. There didn't appear to be any significant familial factor for him being a writer. His parents - and as far as he knew, his grandparents - showed no particular artistic or creative disposition, or even any particular interest in the arts generally.

Out of Stephen's engagement with Kirknane through his writing came his novel - *The Fugitive* - about a political prisoner who escapes from prison and evades re-capture by living in the nearby hills. The novel had great significance to Stephen, for he saw the fugitive as himself, the situation of the fugitive in his community as that of his own situation in Kirknane, and the oppressive nature of the community the fugitive escapes from as that of Kirknane itself. He also sensed that the novel had significance for the community of Kirknane as well.

Stephen saw that the novel could make people see the failings of Kirknane as a society, explain and vindicate his situation in the community and, by thus changing their understanding of the community and of him, allow him his proper place in it. Also that, written in the style of the older literature, the novel's contemporary relevance and the sheer quality of his writing could restore an appreciation of that older literature.

However, because it was written in that style, when Stephen had completed his novel and submitted it to all the publishers of fiction, he did not expect it to be accepted by any of them. He submitted it as a kind of protest in which they would have to acknowledge its existence as well as read and consciously reject it. In doing so, moreover, he would also have gained a very small but significant readership for his novel.

Stephen had since received from all the publishers the letters of rejection he had expected. However, the one from Davina Corrie, commissioning editor at a publishers in Kirknane itself called Blackburns, nonetheless recognised his potential and for that reason invited him to meet her briefly for her to offer some 'helpful guidance'. Stephen accepted the invitation, but only because he did not know what to do next with his novel and intuitively thought that meeting Corrie as suggested might somehow help him in that regard in some unintended way on her part.

Three

It took about twenty minutes for Stephen to get from his home to the offices of Blackburns the publishers. Pausing outside, he checked his watch: he was there on time. He entered the building and spoke to the receptionist then followed her directions to Davina Corrie's office. It was an old building, built of stone, and with its dull lighting had a dark and cavernous aura. Eventually, Stephen found a door with 'Davina Corrie - Commissioning Editor' on it. He knocked on the door then half entered, keeping hold of the door handle, to find a woman sitting behind her desk and looking up at him expectantly.

'Davina Corrie?'

'Yes.'

'Hello, my name is Stephen Whyte. I have an appointment with you at 11.15.'

'Hello Stephen, come right in.'

Stephen closed the door behind him and approached Corrie as she rose from behind her desk to greet him.

'Pleased to meet you Stephen.'

'Pleased to meet you too.'

They shook hands and exchanged smiles (the informality of their introduction to each other was a mark of Kirknane's egalitarianism).

'Please take a seat,' said Corrie, and they sat down on opposite sides of her desk.

She then spent a few moments searching through one of her desk drawers before pulling out a bundle of paper. As Stephen watched her, he immediately sensed that she was an agent of the community's power.

'Here we are,' she declared, and placed in front of her on the desk what Stephen recognised as his manuscript. It felt strange to him to see it that way: such a personal thing in the possession of a stranger - despite him having sent it, and to other publishers.

Before speaking, Corrie spent a few moments reading a note in her own handwriting that was attached to the cover of the manuscript.

'Well Stephen, as you know from my letter, I'm sorry to say that your novel isn't suitable for us for several reasons. However, I think you have the potential to be a good writer so I have invited you here today to try and help guide you a little for any future efforts by explaining the problems with *The Fugitive*.'

She paused for a moment before beginning her critique.

'The first thing is the lack of action. The first three chapters are good, but after that - once the main character reaches the hills - nothing seems to happen, and there is no real ending. A novel should have an eventful story all the way through with some sort of conflict to be resolved, and a good ending to tie everything up.

'Another thing is that the main character lacks some of the qualities that our readers expect, and like to identify with, in such a person - for example, he lacks dynamism and decisiveness. There is also no sign of the friends who should be helping him, or any romantic interest, which makes him come across as cold and aloof. (It's not *always* essential, but our readers do like - expect even - a romantic interest). Overall, therefore, your main character is not the kind our readers would take to. A main character dealing properly with the events and conflict he should encounter, and with the help of friends and a supportive romantic interest, would bring out the admirable qualities that he needs to display.

'Also, your character doesn't seem to have any compelling reason for being a fugitive; his fugitive status seems to be simply self-justification for his behaviour. If a main character is to be a fugitive or something similar, then it must be for a good reason - like a result of some sort of accidental injustice. Nor does your main character seek help from the authorities in any way to resolve his problem, yet this would be the natural and proper behaviour of any citizen - and that could form the ending that your novel lacks.

'The last thing is your choice of words and the way you use them. You often use long and unusual words and write them in long and involved sentences. This makes the novel difficult to read, and it gets worse as the novel goes on as if to make up for the lack of anything happening. You need to make a story easy and enjoyable to read by using shorter, simpler words that your readers are comfortably familiar with, and in shorter, simpler sentences.

'These are the problems with your writing of this novel. As it stands it would not be successful with our readership, and my first responsibility is to them. As I said, however, I think you have potential and if you follow my guidance I think you could well be a successful writer. What do you think?'

Stephen knew he could not follow Corrie's guidance and therefore whatever potential he had was not going to be realised by Davina Corrie or Blackburns the publishers. All he had got from the meeting so far was a detailed confirmation of the impossibility of getting his novel published that the straightforward, tersely worded rejection letters he had received from the publishers he had submitted his novel to had not provided. That confirmation had come at a price, however. Up till now his novel had been solely his own creation, and one that he had nurtured daily - for two years - from conception to what he considered its completion when he was finally completely satisfied with it. Stephen was proud of that achievement and treasured his novel. Now Corrie, after only three weeks - at most - of knowing it, had comprehensively dismissed it – or worse, rewritten it - on her own terms, and he had had to sit there politely listening to her as she did so. Nonetheless, he had yet to get from the meeting any indication or suggestion, however intended or not by Corrie, of what to do next with his novel, and it was the anticipation of this that had brought him here, so to that end Stephen would politely maintain the fiction of his interest in her guidance for its own sake.

'Well firstly, thanks for taking the time to meet me. Thank you also for recognising my potential. I understand and appreciate your guidance, but I do have real concerns about how true to myself as a writer I would be if I followed your guidance.'

'Don't worry,' Corrie assured him, 'your concerns are quite typical for an unpublished writer. However, if you want to be published - if you want to be a *proper* author - you must overcome these concerns to some extent at least. Writing a novel begins as an individual effort, but getting it into the hands of the reading public, and to be the best it can be, is a group effort. We publishers are on your side, for we want - and do - the best for you as a writer. Trust me, I've been doing this job for twenty years! Besides, you don't want to waste your talent; you must share it with the rest of the community!'

With that the meeting was essentially over, for neither Stephen nor Corrie had anything more of significance to say. They soon said their goodbyes to each other then Stephen left Corrie's office, and made his way home.

Four

On the way home from his meeting with Davina Corrie, Stephen spent the time thinking about what she had said, and as soon as he got home he made himself some coffee then went to sit at his bedroom window to continue with his thoughts.

Stephen was not surprised at Corrie's criticism of his novel because its 'problems' as she saw them were the problems of his own place in the community. The main character's attributes and conduct were that of his own attributes and conduct in Kirknane, and such a character could not, therefore, have the qualities that Corrie wanted. The main character's existence in the hills – which formed the story line of the novel - was uneventful and had no clear ending because Stephen's own existence in Kirknane was one of unresolved, and seemingly unresolvable, passive withdrawal from the community. Stephen's writing style, that Corrie had criticised as being too difficult in structure and vocabulary, was a reflection of his preference for the writing style of the older literature and its better qualities of expression, and his aversion to the contemporary style of writing.

It was now absolutely and explicitly clear to Stephen that in order to be published - to be published at all - he must write according to Corrie's guidance, and in all its aspects. This he could not do. Her exposition of how *The Fugitive* should have been written made him realise just how fundamentally different and wrong it would be if written in accordance with her guidance, and the same would apply to any other writing he did. It would also mean him endorsing the community life that he had steadfastly rejected for all its wrongs, and renouncing his own way of life - one he had constructed and maintained, at considerable personal cost, because of its rightness. He would be surrendering to the power of the community. Despite his frustration at not being able to get his novel published, he was glad he had not so surrendered and had retained the power – albeit latent – of his novel. He remained certain of his vocation as a writer, of his writing ability, of the rightness of his novel in all its aspects, and that his novel had some purpose for the betterment of the community of Kirknane. However, if there was a means of him resolving his predicament of having a novel he could not get published but needed to be published, he did not have even an inkling of what it was. He had certainly not got the idea of what to do next with his novel that he had anticipated getting from his meeting with Corrie, which had been his real motivation for seeing her.

Stephen now felt all the more rejected, alienated, frustrated and conflicted with the community. Consequently, he now felt all the more angry and now simply wanted to escape Kirknane and his place in it.

Five

Stephen had just left his flat and was walking along his street. The whole length of the street formed part of Kirknane's border with the adjacent countryside, but with tenements running almost continuously along both sides he could not actually see anything of that countryside until, a few hundred metres from his home, he reached a gap. The gap was the asphalted part of a loan that gave access to the adjoining farm and its fields. Stephen made his way down the loan. Once he was past the tenements and their back greens on either side of him, the loan became a track of compacted stones and earth with grass running down the middle of it. Stephen was now entering the same countryside he looked out on from his bedroom window.

Stephen was impelled by the piece of paper he carried with him in his jacket pocket and that he had already touched to make sure it was still there. He had torn it out the 'Situations Vacant' section of the latest edition of the Kirknane Advertiser, Kirknane's newspaper – the job adverts were the main reason for his buying it, for he was usually dissatisfied with his existing job and looking for something better. It was an advert placed by the Kirknane Water Company for a new water operative. The pay and conditions as outlined in the advert were similar to what Stephen were used to and was not what interested him. What had commanded his attention was the statement that, after training, the successful applicant would spend the following six months working at the reservoir that supplied Kirknane with all its water needs and, because it was so isolated and required constant attendance, would stay there for the entire six months uninterrupted – and alone. As soon as he had seen the advert Stephen excitedly saw his escape from Kirknane.

However, his initial excitement had soon given way to doubts. He knew if he got the job and went to the reservoir it would be a testing experience for him. The prospect of extreme isolation that attracted him also made him concerned about his ability to cope with it, for he was more dependent on the community than he usually liked to admit. He was also unsure if going to the reservoir was the right thing to do in any case, for he saw it as a means of escaping from his situation in Kirknane rather than confronting and resolving it as he knew he should.

Thus, Stephen left for the countryside to emulate, as much as he could, being physically and mentally separated from Kirknane in the hope it might help him to resolve his doubts. Though he had ventured out like this a few times in the past, it was so long ago and in circumstances so different that those experiences were neither easy to recall nor in any case that helpful. On those occasions, as today, he had left very early in the morning before people would generally be up and about - especially any farm workers - and sneaked out of the town like some fugitive. Walking in the countryside was simply not the done thing and would be regarded as somewhat strange, if not suspicious, behaviour if it was noticed, and all the more so for someone on their own. The community prided itself on how successfully and virtuously self-contained it was, and saw no need for anyone to get away from it for however long. The measures therefore necessary to avoid detection, such as going at abnormal hours and maintaining a constant vigilance, had made such trips seem to Stephen not usually worth the risks involved. They could never be spontaneous or carefree, and he had a troubled enough standing in Kirknane as it was. Such restrictions and their effect on his current trip added to his desire to go to the reservoir.

As Stephen made his way along the loan, he came to a field gate to one side of it and decided to pause there for a while. He shouldn't really stop that close to the town for fear of being spotted and identified, but on this particular trip he had something of a devil-may-care attitude. Though somewhat out of character, he found it quite exhilarating for it felt positive and liberating. He went up to the gate and leant against it by resting his arms on the top bar. In this position, he now looked back towards Kirknane for the first time on his walk. He identified his flat and the bedroom window he sat at every day, and then looked at all the other windows facing him. He wondered how much notice their owners took of the countryside they could see from them (the same view as his own from his bedroom window) and, if they did take any notice, what they made of what they saw - he suspected they hardly took any notice at all and made little or nothing of what they saw: their windows being merely a device for providing a utilitarian light. Admittedly, the view from the windows could seem to be unchanging and unimportant, except for allowing a quick check of the weather before venturing outside, but every day Stephen used his view almost instinctively as a means of concentrating when sitting at his bedroom window thinking about things. In order to settle his naturally inquisitive mind before such thinking, he would first observe what had changed in his view – usually the weather – since last looking out. In this way, he closely observed the changing picture, the changing light, of the view through his window. Then, as if provoked by his dismissive thought about how others used, or rather didn't use, their own view, someone appeared at one of the windows Stephen was looking at and gave him something of a start. His devil-may-care attitude vanished at the suddenly real prospect of being spotted and identified, and he felt uneasy enough to want further away immediately. He left the gate he was standing at and continued along the loan.

After a while, at another gate some distance from the one he had left, Stephen stopped again and looked back towards Kirknane. He now felt a safer distance from the town: much less likely to be spotted, far less identified, should anyone look out towards him, and he couldn't see the person at their window he had seen earlier.

Stephen took a relaxed look about him. He was surrounded by cultivated fields that were bounded by semi-wild hedgerows. The hedgerows were occasionally punctuated with field gates like the one he now stood at. In the corner of one field was a small piece of uncultivated land, its wildness intact, in seeming victory against the community's intentions for it. Overall, he sensed this was a meeting-place for two opposing forces, nature and Kirknane, where neither fully held sway. To Stephen, this sense of the nature that surrounded him as an alternative and sometimes opposing force to the community made him feel stronger and less isolated. It was as if he had found an ally in his conflict with the community.

The thought struck him that the reservoir posting offered the same such positive and supportive environment, rather than hostile isolation, and for six months rather than fleeting minutes. Moreover, instead of the worry of avoiding detection, it could be experienced spontaneously and in a carefree manner. He also thought how just as this brief trip getting away from Kirknane was helping him resolve an issue, so the reservoir posting, making him free and detached from his life in Kirknane, could help him all the more to confront himself with his situation in Kirknane and develop a means to resolve it – to see it in a different light. Then he thought of the propitious timing of the job vacancy coming up - something he gave great significance to - and this in turn evoked a certain sense of mission he had experienced ever since he first started writing.

It began raining gently, with little drops falling on his head that felt to him like little nudges of encouragement, for it was the same such rain that filled the reservoir. Stephen needed no more persuasion, for now he believed he could cope with a six month posting to the reservoir on his own, and could better confront his situation in Kirknane there. He decided to apply for the job.

Then, as if waiting for his decision, the rain began to fall more heavily and became less comfortable for him. With his mind made up, there was now no reason for him to stay out in the rain, and his seat at his bedroom window became enticing once again. He turned for home rekindled with the enthusiasm he had felt when he first read the job advert.

Six

Despite the journey's somewhat forbidding reputation among his fellow water operatives, Stephen was enjoying driving to the reservoir. The route was a rough track that went up and down and round and about as it followed the topography of the land. Though driving one of the Kirknane Water Company's all-terrain vehicles, it seemed to Stephen that he was experiencing every bump and hollow in the track. However, moving, and being moved about, in this way made him feel connected to the land he was driving through in a way that he found unexpectedly satisfying, and pleasingly different from the norm of roads made smooth with asphalt and built as flat and straight as possible. Moreover, as he drove through a landscape he had never seen before, he found so much that was interesting and pleasing to see - and enhanced by it being a beautiful January day that was crisply cold but crisply sunny as well. The hills and their valleys had an intriguing beauty to Stephen and he took a particular delight in the meandering rivers that seemed to accompany him on his journey as they shared the valley floors – there was no river in Kirknane, just a couple of burns that had their courses straightened, taking unnatural right angles, to follow urban boundaries. Every so often a change in the route would give him a new viewpoint and on a couple of occasions, when he was going from one valley to another, he had been presented with an entirely new and wonderful vista, and all the time moving between light and shadow. Intensified by his feelings of escape and freedom from Kirknane, Stephen found the whole experience quite exhilarating, and gave him a childlike sense of innocent wonder and enjoyment.

As his vehicle was jolted by the bumps and hollows of the track, what Stephen had packed in the back was moved about a little, and sometimes made enough noise to remind him of some of what he was bringing. Before he had left Kirknane his new colleagues had given him things of their own that had helped them get by in their own time at the reservoir. Stephen knew he was not likely to use much of it, but out of politeness, a genuine sense of gratitude, and a fear of becoming the 'odd one out' once again, he had accepted every offering with thanks and made a display of putting them in the back of his vehicle. Likewise, he had listened attentively to every bit of advice he was given regardless of how much at variance it was with his own intentions and expectations. The dominant theme of all the support he was proffered was to live largely indoors as if he hadn't really left Kirknane, so unpleasant was the reservoir experience - so much so it was regarded as a final test and rite of passage for a new recruit before acceptance as a 'true' water operative.

Thus, ironically in a job he had taken expressly to distance himself from the community of Kirknane, the perceived adversity of the posting to the reservoir had given Stephen a sense of camaraderie at work that he had never experienced before, and as he drove ever further away from Kirknane and ever deeper into the uninhabited hills that contained the reservoir, the more he appreciated that camaraderie. Stephen also began to better understand the difference between being detached from the community but present in it, and the complete isolation of his new situation.

How tame his walk into the countryside with the torn out job advert now seemed, and how long ago it now felt. He had applied straight away and, interviewed two weeks later, given the job the same day. He was not aware of any other applicants and would not be surprised if he was the only one, given the unattractive nature - to others at least - of the reservoir posting. Indeed, he had wondered if they had given him the job as quickly as possible to pre-empt him changing his mind about wanting it. This had caused him to question his eagerness, but he had quickly reassured himself he was doing the right thing.

Suddenly, Stephen caught his first glimpse of the reservoir and in the excitement all his existing thoughts instantly evaporated - Kirknane had no expanse of water of any kind and was a considerable distance from the sea, so the reservoir was a new experience for him in more ways than one. As he wended his way along the track, the reservoir came in and out of view but his focus on it remained constant: when it was not in sight he looked for it coming back into view. He had developed great expectations for his stay at the reservoir and was eager to see the scene of such anticipation.

Eventually Stephen could see the entire reservoir and its surroundings, including its concrete dam and, adjacent to it, the small cottage he would be staying in and the even smaller works building he would be partly working in. Not knowing how quickly his predecessor would leave, he stopped the vehicle before he reached the buildings, switched off the engine and got out, so he could briefly view the whole place alone and in silence before he met the incumbent operative. He stood in front of the vehicle and surveyed the scene before him. The reservoir was so placid that its surface was smooth to an almost eerie degree. In its alluring depths he could sense a profound and mysterious otherness. The surrounding hills that gave the reservoir its shape were plainly clad with grass and heather, and devoid of little else except for some clumps of trees around the edge of the reservoir, but had a curiously pleasing aspect. The sky had a lovely bright, bluish hue. There was no wind at all, but an utter calm. Only then did Stephen become conscious of how quiet the place was. The combined effect exuded a compelling, almost hypnotic, sense of tranquility. His first experience of the reservoir, and the journey he had experienced to get to it, had not only met but exceeded his expectations and, so far at least, vindicated his decision to come.

Then he saw the incumbent water operative emerge from the cottage with some luggage, presumably having seen or heard Stephen approaching in his vehicle. The man placed his luggage on the ground, where he no doubt expected Stephen to stop the vehicle, then returned inside the front porch of the cottage only to re-emerge quickly after with more luggage. He had evidently already assembled it all in the porch in anticipation of Stephen's arrival in order to return to Kirknane as soon as possible.

Stephen got back in the vehicle, restarted the engine, and completed his journey by driving to the buildings where the track ended and the man now awaited him.

Seven

Stephen's home while at the reservoir was a rather plain, single storey cottage with a kitchen, a living room, a bedroom and a bathroom. Its furniture, fittings and décor were somewhat aged, but sufficiently modern to make for a tolerable stay. It had something of a cold and impersonal atmosphere, however, due largely to its use as temporary accommodation for a succession of different occupants who did not treat it like a home.

To begin with, Stephen had felt uncomfortably alone and isolated, for he was a long way from the nearest person and without any transport – in accordance with the normal practice, the vehicle he used to get to the reservoir was used by the incumbent operative to return to Kirknane - and he was unlikely to see anyone from the Water Company until his replacement came in six months time. Stephen had lived in Kirknane as if he was similarly alone, despite his neighbours being so close that he shared walls with them, but he now understood how little he was truly alone there compared to the utter isolation of the reservoir. He surprised himself with how much he missed having neighbours. Nonetheless, he soon became acclimatised to his isolation and he felt a kinship with the detached solitude of the reservoir. Unlike his fellow operatives, he made no attempt to live at the reservoir as if he was still in Kirknane. It was true there was a barrenness to the place, so he could understand how the others found it so bleak, and resorted to staying in the cottage as much as possible, but to him the reservoir and its setting had an austere beauty. Even the concrete dam had a positive effect on him: the simple and plain, but dramatic and expansive way it contained the great volume of the water of the reservoir had a primal yet graceful quality that seemed in tune with its environment. It was the first time Stephen had appreciated any example of Kirknane architecture.

At the reservoir, Stephen was released from his mental and physical combat with the community of Kirknane. As the stress and tension of that combat dissipated, he discovered a calmness, a serenity even, that he had never experienced before. It was only now he could fully appreciate just how stressful was his life in Kirknane and he vowed to try and maintain his new found serenity once he returned there.

Stephen soon settled into his work at the reservoir. His predecessor had given him the most cursory of inductions in order to leave as soon as possible, but Stephen had been glad to be so quickly free of the man's palpable negativity towards the place. In any case, the work was straightforward enough and he had been well trained. His main responsibility was to monitor the reservoir's water quality as well as to be a general caretaker. The monitoring involved taking daily samples of the water at various set points around the reservoir then testing the samples in the works building - a small and very utilitarian structure of concrete walls and corrugated tin roof.

The monitoring work was not very demanding and allowed Stephen most of the day as free time. Every morning he would walk all the way round the reservoir to collect the required water samples - something he always enjoyed. Once back from his walk he would immediately test the samples he had taken.

Stephen got great satisfaction from the responsibility of his job at the reservoir and the trust he was thereby given. The safety and overall quality of the whole of Kirknane's water supply lay considerably with him and him alone. He could not help seeing the irony in how, because of this, this remote and isolated posting made him feel a part of the community in a way and to an extent he had never experienced when living in Kirknane itself.

In this initial period of settling in, Stephen's stay at the reservoir had continued to satisfy his expectations, and he had intuitively become increasingly confident that his time at the reservoir would help him with his situation in Kirknane.

Eight

Once Stephen had completed his daily task of testing the water quality, he would go and sit out at a particular spot that had soon become his favourite place because of the view it gave of the reservoir. Ever since the day he had first seen it, the reservoir had continued to captivate him: the simple beauty and peacefulness of its setting, the quietness that was only interrupted by the sound of the water being released from the dam into the river below and the occasional cry of a bird (and both sounds somehow enhanced the quiet and compelling prospect of its surface - especially when tranquil); its alluring sense of a profound and mysterious depth; its beguiling otherness; its sense of possibility, of a reality far greater than Kirknane, and of an isolation that put Kirknane in its true scale. It also seemed to Stephen that the light at the reservoir had a special clarity that helped him in his reflections as if it gave him the same special clarity within. These were all qualities that he found highly conducive to his contemplations there.

When Stephen first started sitting out at this favoured spot he had simply wrapped himself up against the cold and rain and stayed for a short while. As the days passed, however, he stayed out for progressively longer periods, and took to taking with him something to eat and drink, and paper and a pen to write down any thoughts he wished to make a note of. Eventually, in order to spend the time there that he wanted to comfortably, he constructed a makeshift shelter. He made it with three solid sides and a roof in order to keep the rain and the cold bearing wind out, but the side facing the reservoir he left open so as to view it easily and still experience the weather. Indeed, whenever conditions were favourable, he would sit just outside the open front of the shelter in order to experience the weather more completely and directly. He loved to feel the weather on him - whether the warmth of the sun, the wetness of the rain, or the blowing of the wind. When conditions got uncomfortable, he would retreat into the refuge of his shelter and its comfortable seating provided by the cushions from the cottage's sofa. Despite its small size and ramshackle construction, Stephen came to look on his shelter with considerable affection and regard because of how it allowed him to engage with the reservoir.

Because of the cold, Stephen would often build a fire just in front of the shelter. He made a circle of large stones and within that would burn some of the wood provided for the cottage's wood burning stove. There was something fundamentally satisfying to Stephen - perhaps because of its elemental nature - in sitting on the earth in front of the fire and contemplating the water of the reservoir in the special light there.

When Stephen came to sit at the shelter for his meditations, he would attune himself to, and absorb, the particular conditions pertaining to his view of the reservoir at that time – his daily circumnavigation of the reservoir to take water samples helped him in this regard. This allowed the natural inquisitiveness of his mind towards its environment to be satisfied. With his mind thus settled, he would begin contemplating the reservoir and let himself be enthralled by its qualities while remaining open to whatever came to mind. He would usually find himself pondering his life in Kirknane – both his past and, attuned to the sense of possibility the reservoir offered, his future.

Nine

In his long hours of meditation at the reservoir, Stephen came to experience a profound revelation. He became aware of the existence of what he saw as a great unseen power within the reservoir. When he humbly and sincerely submitted his thoughts to it, the answers and understandings that he sought came to him - although the timing and circumstances of those answers and understandings varied and did not usually occur straight away or while actually contemplating the reservoir. He found that the more passive and submissive he was in this practice, the better, more dynamic, was the response he received, and that his clarity of thought had a likewise clarity of response. The more he attuned himself to it, both in his enquiries and more generally, the better he came to understand it; and the more familiar it became to him, the easier it became to invoke. He came to see that it was not nature itself but operated in nature, and that it was not in itself material but operated through material things. He came to realise that it had a personality and that he was developing a relationship with it: it was becoming something like an intimate companion. He also found it a somewhat paradoxical power, for it was both personal and impersonal, and both constant and ever-changing. The elusive, multi-faceted and paradoxical nature of the power made it difficult for him to give it a meaningful, adequate name, so he decided just to call it 'the Power.' He sensed that it was the power he had experienced in nature in his trip to the countryside. The reservoir seemed to him to be either a concentration of this power or its source.

Despite his apparent discovery of the Power at the reservoir, Stephen knew it was not wholly new to him. He had met and used the Power before, but had only now become truly aware of it. He now saw that his sessions of contemplating the reservoir were to some extent simply a more intense form of him staring out of his bedroom window as he thought about things; in particular in regard to his writing. He realised that, from that window, he had been staring towards the reservoir all that time: perhaps it was drawing him to it even then. He also now realised that the Power had already manifested itself in his inspiration to write, and in the sensibility of his writing, as well as in the writing of the older literature of Kirknane and his reading of it.

In his realisation of the Power, and his engagement with it,

Stephen became aware of a subtle and sublime life of the world that the Power animated. He also saw that the Power and its life had a beautiful truth and virtue, and in the light of that truth and virtue everything counter to it was clearly exposed in all its wrongness.

Just as Stephen's realisation of the Power, and engagement with it, enriched and transformed his time at the reservoir and himself, so he could see how such a realisation of the Power, and engagement with it, by the people of Kirknane could enrich and transform the life of the community and everyone in it. Indeed, he could now see it was the very lack of this that gave Kirknane its awful condition. The Power had been lost save for him, and after him would be completely lost – irrecoverably? – from Kirknane. These thoughts gave Stephen the idea that he must somehow pass on an awareness and knowledge of the Power to others in Kirknane so that it would both survive him and transform the community for the better. This, in turn, made him wonder if he had been sent into a wilderness like some ancient prophet he had read about in the older literature, to return to his community with their salvation.

Ten

When Stephen's novel was rejected by all the publishers he had submitted it to, he stopped writing altogether. During the course of his application for the water operative job and his subsequent training, he continued not writing. His experiences at the reservoir, however, inspired him to start again. It began with a few phrases or lines coming to him unforced, but insistently. In these first words and lines, he saw the embryonic manifestation of a particular work that he intuitively sensed had significance. He started mixing and matching them into what seemed their inherent structure. This was how his novel had first been formed. This time, however, it was a poem that emerged rather than a novel. The poem was about the enchantment of the reservoir and the Power. Stephen soon came to call the poem *The Reservoir*.

At first, this change from prose to poetry surprised and somewhat perplexed Stephen, for he had never written poetry before or taken that much interest in it. However, as he worked on his poem he saw that it could operate with a directness, intensity and sublimeness that his prose could not, and its concision relative to prose made it more accessible. *The Reservoir* developed into a means in itself of invoking the Power. This would allow others in Kirknane to share Stephen's experience of the reservoir and the Power, and without needing to go to the reservoir itself.

As Stephen developed his poem, he drew considerably on his novel in various ways. His novel now revealed its true significance, for his writing of it and his failure to get it published had led him to the reservoir and the revelation of the Power, and this in turn had led him to poetry and *The Reservoir*. He wouldn't have written the poem if he had stayed in Kirknane, for he had to come here first, driven by his novel and having it to draw on. This was the true purpose of his novel and, having been accomplished, he must now discard it. He had already discarded earlier drafts of his novel to allow it to develop. He had seen this as being like an animal discarding its old skin for a new one that would allow further growth. He now saw the change from prose to poetry as a metamorphosis from the pupa of his novel to the imago of his poem. His frustration with, and concerns for, his novel were now replaced with a gladdening satisfaction at his final realisation of its true significance and purpose.

Stephen decided that when he returned to Kirknane he would

submit *The Reservoir* to *Words* poetry magazine. With his aversion to contemporary literature and his hitherto preference for prose, he had largely ignored this magazine that was the sole outlet for poetry in Kirknane. Moreover, from the few occasions he had tried reading it, it seemed to him to be the preserve of dilettantes - in contrast to his own vocation as a serious writer. It also seemed to him to be mainly read by its contributors. Stephen expected *The Reservoir* to be rejected by the editor of *Words*, just as *The Fugitive* had been rejected by Davina Corrie, and end up with the same problem getting it published in the community, but he thought he should test the possibility in any case. Moreover, its rejection might be significant in itself just as the rejection of his novel was.

Even if *The Reservoir* was published in *Words* Stephen knew it would only directly affect a relative few, but he wanted to reach the whole community. Indeed, that want had by now become a responsibility. As the water operative at the reservoir, he was responsible for providing the life-giving qualities of water to Kirknane - to irrigate the community physically, including their bodies. Now he was responsible for providing the life-giving qualities of the Power to Kirknane - to irrigate the community mentally. His inspiration as a writer was a manifestation of the Power. It had irrigated his own arid life in Kirknane into a fertile one – in particular in the cultivation of his novel. Now he must lead the community to their own realisation of, and engagement with, the Power. To Stephen, it was in one sense a tremendously daunting task and yet, seeing Kirknane in its true scale to the magnitude and potency of the Power, he was confident it was achievable.

However, he still had doubts over the whole thing. Was he fooling himself? Was he simply easing his return to Kirknane by giving himself a compelling and positive reason for going back? Was it a clever way of engaging and socialising with the rest of the community without having to change or sacrifice his own personality and lifestyle? Was he switching to poetry simply because he couldn't get his novel published?

Eleven

Stephen's posting at the reservoir finally came to an end. In the morning of his departure, he made his last circuit of the reservoir, followed by his final testing of water samples he had collected, then sat at his favoured spot for the last time. The usual pleasures of these experiences were naturally impaired by the knowledge that they would be the last ones for a long time. He had at least managed to restrict such despondency more or less to this day, for with some effort he had succeeded in keeping previous days relatively normal and happy – even yesterday (which was a measure of the positive effect of the Power on him).

After his last session of contemplation, Stephen reluctantly demolished his treasured shelter and removed all trace of it. He knew how circumspect he must be to achieve his aims, so he must minimise as much as possible any overt indications of weirdness that might alienate those he sought to reach. Removing any sign of his shelter was therefore necessary for, in order to extend his mission beyond getting *The Reservoir* published and read, he had decided to engage with the other water operatives. They had all worked and stayed at the reservoir just as he had, so they should be more receptive to his message than others. He did not want any success with the other operatives to be undone in six months time by his replacement returning to Kirknane with damaging evidence regarding his stay at the reservoir. Due largely to the shortness of his initial training period and his immediate posting to the reservoir on his own, he had so far managed to avoid coming across as weird to his co-workers in the way he was apt to.

Once Stephen had finished packing his things and cleaning the accommodation, he sat outside and awaited his replacement. He had one last look at the reservoir on his own. It was difficult for him to accept that it could be a matter of years before he returned. He held on to the slight hope that for some reason a substitute might be needed - perhaps someone falling ill or finding the isolation too much (such an inappropriate thought from an exponent of the Power!). Under such a circumstance he was confident he would be the only one to volunteer.

The replacement arrived pretty much at the time expected. There was no need to familiarise him with the place for he had worked at the reservoir before. They both unloaded the vehicle he had arrived in and reloaded it with Stephen's things. They each took their time, for Stephen was in no hurry to leave and his replacement was happy for the company before six months on his own.

The matter of fact demeanour of his replacement, and the fact of never having really spoken to him before, made it difficult for Stephen to speak to him as he had planned, for he intended beginning his mission among the water operatives with this very first opportunity. He first wanted to find out if his fellow operatives, starting with his replacement, had experienced the Power in the reservoir in any kind of way he had. It was only when he was finally about to leave that he exploited a chance. He tried to make what he said sound as spontaneous, reasonable and normal as possible.

'Well that was some experience,' he said, 'what do you make of this place?'

The newly arrived water operative, however, failed to respond in a way that would allow Stephen to develop his initial approach easily, but simply made some banal comment about the reservoir of the kind Stephen had heard from the other operatives before leaving for the reservoir himself, and with a finality that he could not counter. With that, the opportunity swiftly passed.

The complete failure of his first effort was a little disappointing but not that surprising, for although he thought approaching someone whilst actually at the reservoir would help to elicit the desired response, he also realised that a replacement operative arriving at the start of a six month stint there might not be best disposed to such an approach - if only he could stay and guide each operative to an experience of the Power during their posting to the reservoir! Nevertheless, there was still the prospect of the opportunities he would have back at Kirknane to speak to the others.

Twelve

Stephen arrived back in Kirknane late at night - as he had intended. All was quiet - as he had hoped. He had delayed his return for as long as possible, driving slowly and stopping often, for he did not want to encounter anyone in Kirknane before settling back into his flat - he made a necessary exception in buying some food and drink at a late-open store. After six happy months on his own at the reservoir, meeting his replacement and going to the store was enough human contact for the day. He could have quite happily stayed at the reservoir for ever, so his fatalism and sense of mission made him suppose the compulsory nature of his return was no accident.

When Stephen finally entered his flat, it was still somewhat light, for it was a June night that would not get particularly dark, if at all, till later. Before him, curtains open, lay the flat as he had left it. He was immediately struck by the stale air and light, for his flat had not been aired for the six months he was away. The contrast with the fresh and invigorating air and light at the reservoir was palpable. He immediately went round all the rooms opening the windows as fully as possible. After that, he went into the kitchen to make himself some coffee with some of the coffee beans he had just bought. He knew the water had been sitting in his pipes for six months and would be as stale as the air and light, so he ran the tap till he was sure fresh water was coming through, and then filled his kettle. How strange, he thought, that the water he was now using was the same water he had been with at the reservoir - a place that now seemed so far away - and had probably come to Kirknane this same day and on a similar journey.

With his cup of coffee made and in hand, Stephen sat down in his chair at his bedroom window. Everything that was once familiar now seemed a little strange. It felt as if the place belonged to someone else, and in a sense it did, for he had returned as a different person from the one that had left six months ago when his flat was familiar and the reservoir a far off, unknown place. What an experience he had had over those last six months! He could not help thinking longingly of his lengthy sessions at his shelter and his walks round the reservoir. Such recollection made his flat feel like a prison cell and Kirknane a kind of open prison - no wonder he had wanted to escape!

As he sat there in his chair, however, Stephen found himself already gradually acclimatising to being back home and, invigorated by the coffee and the fresh air wafting in through the window and refreshing the light, his mood became more positive. He decided that sitting at his open bedroom window, with fresh air coming in and – in the daytime – an often clear and unspoilt view of the hills that held the reservoir, helped make Kirknane bearable enough and something of a likeness to being in his shelter. He also had *The Reservoir* to invoke the Power. Furthermore, he had his mission in the community to concentrate on, and he knew its success meant the Power operating in Kirknane and thus transforming his and everyone else's life here. Amongst other things, it would allow him to go into the countryside around Kirknane in the same carefree manner of his daily circuit of the reservoir. Moreover, if he was honest with himself, he would have to admit that he felt a little *too* isolated at the reservoir and was not completely unhappy at returning to what, after all, was his home. He also now had a better appreciation of human company!

Stephen contemplated his next posting. He would spend the next six months in the office at the Water Company depot - the six month rotation of water operatives to the reservoir in turn led to all other postings being rotated for the same length of time. The depot posting - considered the best - always followed the reservoir one - considered the worst. It was both a reward and an incentive for operatives completing the six months at the reservoir. It was seen as the least arduous one as it was one of support for the others when the need arose. This was something which apparently happened infrequently - though often enough for Stephen's intentions. Most of the time was seemingly spent in the office simply being available while idling the time away or, if so inclined, indolently helping the office staff. More importantly for Stephen, it was the only posting that allowed an operative to meet with the others at work, for all the other postings were solitary in nature. Because of this,˙ it was an ideal opportunity for him to pursue his mission in the way he had planned: to engage with all the other operatives about his and their experience of the reservoir and the Power.

Once again he was struck by the auspicious nature, including its timeliness, of his work. With that concluding thought, and feeling rather tired, he finished the last of his coffee and went to bed.

Thirteen

Stephen woke up and immediately remembered he had another day in the office at the Water Company's depot. He would stay in bed until he had to get up. First he recited *The Reservoir* to invoke the Power - he had begun performing this invocation first thing every morning before engaging with the coming day (although this didn't change other people or his situation, it made him more tolerant and forgiving of others' transgressions). Then he listened out for the postman with the early morning post. He had done this for some days now, for according to *Words* magazine they would respond to submissions within three months and it was now almost three months since he had returned to Kirknane and submitted his poem. It was a sign of the mundanity of his life now he was back in Kirknane that he waited in this manner despite not expecting his poem to be accepted for publication. Those three months since he had been at the reservoir felt to him like it had been far longer, and he reckoned it would be another three years or so before he returned there. In the meantime he must continue his work as a water operative in Kirknane.

If Stephen did not get a reply this morning it would be a typical day at the depot office. He did not look forward to such a day. Instead of the pleasures of a serene walk around the reservoir, followed by a long and rewarding session of contemplation at his shelter, he would walk through Kirknane to the depot and sit at his desk for most of the day. He would be trapped in an airless office lit by artificial light, for his co-workers liked all the windows kept fully shut and all the lights kept on, regardless of the opportunity for fresh air or fresh natural light. Instead of silence there would be a constant chatter from other people, and he would be expected to join in to some extent at least. He could see the sky from the window next to his desk, and would like to be able to observe the clouds, but such behaviour would be considered strange. Any attempt to go against the norm would be greeted with strong disapproval and perhaps hostility. Not wanting that to happen, not wanting to endanger the possible success of his mission in that way, he would, as before, go along with it all. It was the very situation that he had always previously tried to avoid, and his experience at the depot now justified such avoidance. Whereas the reservoir posting was supposed to be a trial and the depot posting a pleasure, it was completely the other way round for him, but he consoled himself with the knowledge that this posting was only for a six month period, and that after it he would be back to working largely on his own and out of any office.

Stephen cast his mind back over the past three months. He had engaged with the other water operatives whenever the somewhat infrequent opportunity had arisen, and probed them about their experience of the reservoir. He had met with disappointing results, however, as none of them gave any indication they had anything resembling his experience of the reservoir and the Power. Moreover, since his return from the reservoir, he was becoming accustomed once again to his life in Kirknane. This concerned him, for he felt he was relapsing into his pre-reservoir accommodation with his situation in the community and that this would undermine his sense of mission. As if in confirmation of this, and not for the first time since his return to Kirknane, he became affected by a sense of the absurdity of his mission, at the sheer scale and nature of it, and by a sense of inadequacy in his ability to achieve it. Could he really do it? Could he really transform the community and everyone in it? How could he personally convert people to the Power when he struggled with even mundane social intercourse that was, relatively, such a small expression of the power of the community?

He was about to ponder these questions further when he was interrupted by the sound of the common door to his tenement open. Old and heavy, it creaked in complaint whenever it was disturbed, and loud enough to be heard by him as he lay in bed. He could now hear someone's steps on the bare stone of the common stair with the sound of each step crisply echoing up to him. Was it the postman? Soon he heard the steps come to a stop, a letterbox being opened, then further steps: it *was* the postman. He continued to listen as slowly but surely the postman approached his flat on the top floor. Eventually the postman arrived at Stephen's front door. He heard his letter box being opened and something put through it landing on his hall floor. He got out of bed and went through to the hall to see what was there. On the floor was a solitary white envelope. He picked it up and examined it. It bore the frank of *Words* magazine. His pulse raced a little as he tore open the envelope. He took out the letter that was inside, unfolded it, and quickly scanned the text for the answer he forlornly hoped for. He saw the words 'regret' and 'not suitable' then, disappointed despite his expectation of rejection, read the letter more closely. It thanked him for his submission and explained how carefully *The Reservoir* had been read, but regretted to say that this particular poem was not suitable for the magazine. The letter ended with the hope that he would submit further work for consideration.

Fourteen

Stephen walked up to the main doors of the building housing Kirknane's swimming pool and pushed at a door handle with the word 'PUSH' prominently displayed on it. The door refused to move, as did the other doors when he tried them also. He was pleased, for the pool was not meant to be open to the public at this time. Only the occasional member of staff would be around: he would have the place almost to himself. He skirted round the outside of the building to the staff entrance and made his way inside.

Stephen had been sent to carry out a routine check of the swimming pool as the water operative whose job it was had not been able to make it. This cheered him up somewhat, for he would be working on his own, and released from the confines and daily trials of the depot office. This cheerfulness was moderated, however, by the failure of his mission to date. Not only had *The Reservoir* been rejected – though as expected - by *Words* magazine, but he had exhausted his approaches to the other water operatives, which had continued to be uncomfortably contrived, and failed to elicit the response he sought. Unable to articulate his reservoir experience in an effective way, the common response of the other water operatives to his approaches was one of incomprehension. There was no shared language: the people of Kirknane were so alienated from the Power that he couldn't express his experience and awareness of it in their language, and his guarded articulation of it in his own words could not be understood by others. A fuller and more explicit articulation in his own language would be so alien in form and meaning to the community that he would not only fail, but he would come across as some kind of weirdo, and thus create an extra obstacle to success. It was his alienation from the community that had allowed him to experience and appreciate the Power but that same alienation obstructed his transmission of it within the community. He had to find a new means, something that was 'of the community,' but what it was he had, as yet, no idea. In the meantime, he was determined to follow the path he had learnt at the reservoir and trust to let the answer emerge in its own way and at its own time, to pursue and stay faithful to his mission as he had resolved so to do on his return to Kirknane.

When Stephen entered the pool hall he was immediately arrested by the prospect before him: the hall was completely empty of people and utterly silent. The large 50 metre long swimming pool was full of water but its surface was absolutely still. Stephen sat down on a pool side bench to appreciate and absorb the somewhat eerie tranquility of the pool and its setting. As he did so, the whole experience was so calming and engaging to him, and the pool itself so alluring and evoking a sense of profundity, mystery and possibility, that despite knowing its shallowness relative to the reservoir he still came to sense the Power in the pool. The pool was another reservoir! An abode of the Power! In Kirknane! Here was what he was looking for!

After basking in this revelation for a while, Stephen wondered why he had he not thought of this before, for it now seemed so obvious that when the water came from the reservoir into the community it might be formed into some kind of reservoir. Was it due to his consuming prejudice against the community that he could not conceive of such a thing already happening here even if its fuller nature was unconsciously brought about and not yet appreciated? Was it a lack of faith in the Power that he did not expect it to be already at work in Kirknane? Was it egotism on his part not to expect the Power in the community without his agency? Whatever the answer, the community had already created its own reservoir. In doing so, albeit unconsciously, it had committed a subversive act against the authority of its own power.

On further reflection, Stephen also surmised that, in the case of the swimming pool at least, the water from the reservoir had integrated successfully with the community in Kirknane without apparently losing its essential nature. This reassured him that he could likewise integrate successfully with the community without sacrificing his own essential nature, something that - throughout his life in Kirknane - he had been afraid would not be the case.

A more pressing issue, however, now faced Stephen: how could he get people to contemplate the pool in the same way as he did to invoke the Power - especially since the pool hall would have to be as empty of people and silent, and the pool as tranquil, as now? He was so preoccupied with this thought that he was unaware of one of the swimming pool staff approaching him. Realising he had been caught staring at the pool in what must have looked like a rather idiotic fashion he blurted out an attempt to mitigate this as the man passed: 'It's a great view.'

The man gave Stephen a somewhat quizzical look but nevertheless replied: 'Yes, it is, it just makes you want to dive in.'

There, in an instant, the next answer that Stephen sought was provided! Faced with the tranquility of the swimming pool and its setting, he wished to contemplate it whereas the passing man wished to use it as intended. He must use such a response to the swimming pool rather than his own, but in a way that would reveal the Power to the people of Kirknane. Just as the reservoir that he used must be an integral part of the community, so the method he used with that reservoir must be an integral part of the community also.

Stephen now felt a great sense of satisfaction. His approach, and his faith in it, was vindicated, and important progress had been made. Moreover, his sense of mission was reinforced with the knowledge that the likelihood of the pool attendant walking past him at that very time, and saying what he needed to hear to provide him his answer, was so low it had to be fate. Indeed, so affected was he by a sense of fate that he wondered if his colleague's non-appearance was not also destined, for it had driven him to the swimming pool today when it, and its setting, was so tranquil, and had led him to the realisation of the swimming pool as a reservoir in the community and abode of the Power.

Fifteen

Today, the day after Stephen's realisation of the swimming pool as a reservoir and abode of the Power, it was open to the public again. Having finished his work for the day, and gone home for a wash and something to eat, Stephen was returning to the pool. In order to determine the exact role of the pool in his mission, and knowing that the answer must lie in its conventional use by the community, he had decided that observing that use was the best initial approach, so he was now coming back this evening purely as a spectator.

Once inside the building, Stephen made his way to the café. It was called 'The Poolside,' for it was literally poolside with no screen or barrier of any kind between it and the pool itself, although there was a gap between the pool and the tables and chairs of the cafe to avoid cafe users getting splashed or slipping on a wet floor.

When Stephen reached the cafe he found that it was fairly quiet. He went to the counter and ordered a coffee. As he waited for his coffee to be made, he surveyed the other customers seated about. With their hair wet and sports bags at their feet, they were evidently pool users having a post-pool refreshment. It looked like he was the only one here as a spectator. Once he had been given his coffee he went over to, and sat at, the table closest to the pool and that gave him the best possible view of what was going on. He was so close, if the comments of the pool users had any significance he was as likely to hear them sitting there as he was in the pool itself, and the smell of the chlorine in the water seemed as pungent as it could be. It made him feel as much a participant as a spectator, so him not entering the water – Stephen did not swim - didn't seem to matter much in the circumstances. With this all being so conducive to his mission, and the circumstance that allowed it being unique to Kirknane, he considered it another example of his fateful good fortune. He settled himself into a relaxed and receptive state in order to observe the pool users. It was a state that was second nature to him after all the days he had spent sitting at his bedroom window and in his shelter at the reservoir.

What first struck Stephen was how few of the people in the pool were actually swimming. Regardless of their age, most folk were essentially playing in the water one way or another, and splashing about and making a lot of noise in the process. To Stephen, this was bad enough in itself for it was certainly not what he was hoping to find but, also, in this somewhat chaotic environment, the few pool users attempting to swim lengths of the pool faced frequent obstruction and interruption of their progress. They were evidently distracted and disturbed in their efforts at swimming by the behaviour of the other pool users. Stephen admired the perseverance of the swimmers and their restraint at not remonstrating with those who were spoiling their swimming. The conduct he witnessed, however, seemed to him for the most part to be the embodiment of what he saw as the worst features of community behaviour. It was variously self-centred, inconsiderate towards others, ignorant of the effect of one's behaviour on others, graceless, unnecessarily noisy... Stephen saw that, once again, Kirknane's ethos of freedom and equality was being used by many as a licence for what he saw as simply bad behaviour. The basic requirements for the sort of swimming experience Stephen hoped to find were lacking, and he found nothing to suggest the way forward.

After some considerable time further contemplating it all without making any progress, Stephen wished to leave. The goings on in the pool had become both quite irritating and disruptive to his thought. He would go home to the quiet solitude of his flat to contemplate the matter further. If necessary, he would come back for the next evening session at the pool, and keep coming back to evening sessions thereafter until the way forward revealed itself. He would keep his faith in his mission and realised method.

He got up from his seat and left the café. As he made his way out the building, he noticed a poster on the wall and for some reason felt compelled to read it. It was an announcement by the Kirknane Swimming Club that the next weekly session had been rearranged from its normal time. Yes! He immediately realised that this was the answer, or the way to the answer, that he was seeking. In a Swimming Club session there would only be true and dedicated swimmers, and there would presumably be none of the baser behaviour he had witnessed this evening that had so inhibited the swimmers. Once again the answer had come and his faith rewarded and justified – and so quickly!

Sixteen

The next session at the swimming pool of the Kirknane Swimming Club was scheduled to start at half past seven that evening, with the pool reserved exclusively for that purpose. The café remained open to the public, however, so Stephen made his way there in order to observe the session. He made sure he was there early enough to witness anything, including anything before the session got properly underway, that might help him in his mission. It was about a quarter past seven, therefore, when he entered the poolside cafe. It had much the same number of customers as had been there on his previous visit when he had observed a public session of the pool. This time, however, the place seemed a little more subdued. As he went to the cafe counter he could see that the pool was empty. To Stephen, this gave the coming session an air of expectation. Having bought a coffee, he sat down at the same table and on the same seat as before.

Stephen looked at the pool: it was the same enchanting prospect he had experienced when he had come to the pool when it was closed. It was not only empty of people but the surface was completely calm and he could sense the presence of the Power. He was delighted not only at this but that the presence of other people this time, albeit few in number, did not prevent the essence of the experience. Though he would have preferred solitude himself, it was clearly not essential, and he supposed that others in the community would find it less important.

Eventually, at roughly half past seven, people began emerging from the unisex changing rooms and making their way to the poolside. They were a diverse mixture of adults and children, male and female, old and young - perhaps twenty people altogether. Compared with the public session that Stephen had attended, the participants seemed to him to be a little solemn and evidently treating the session they were taking part in with some seriousness. No-one entered the pool itself at this point but, instead, everyone gathered themselves into two groups: one consisting of the adults and one consisting of the children. After a short while two adults appeared; both were fully dressed in sports clothing and both were bearing a clipboard. One went to where the adult group was assembled and began addressing them while the other one went to the children's group and began addressing the children. Soon after, the adult group took to the water on one side of the pool, using a set of steps attached to the inside of the pool, while the children's group made their way to the other side of the pool and entered the water using a similar set of steps. Once in the water, both groups remained separated from each other and with their respective members still assembled together. It seemed to Stephen as if the pool had been divided lengthways between the two groups, but without using any overt physical means - unless, he supposed, they were guided by the lane markings that were painted on the floor of the pool. Even though they had done nothing more so far than entering the water, he was pleased by what he had seen in the attitude and conduct of the Swimming Club members compared to the pool users in the public session.

Over the next hour or so, Stephen watched the two groups going through their activities. Both groups followed the same pattern of instruction in technique alternating with applying that instruction in swimming lengths of the pool. He could tell by hearing what the instructors were saying to the swimmers that the reason for improving their technique was to improve their speed for the purpose of competition. At the end of their instruction, the swimmers within each group then raced against each other over varying numbers of lengths of the pool with the instructors timing them. The swimmers then left the pool en-masse and headed for the changing rooms. There was a buzz about them now, evidently buoyed by their session, with them talking enthusiastically and happily to each other.

Stephen got himself another cup of coffee, then returned to his seat to mull over his observations and thoughts about the session he had just witnessed. He had mixed impressions of it all.

On the positive side, the session had begun with the pool empty of people and undisturbed. This not only gave a sense of anticipation and occasion but, more importantly was an opportunity for the swimmers to be affected by that prospect as Stephen was, to experience the presence of the Power. The session was organised and disciplined, and with an evident sense that everyone in the pool had a common, shared purpose. Individually the swimmers were invariably quiet, serious, considerate and disciplined - there was none of the noisy, erratic and disruptive behaviour that Stephen had experienced at the public session. Since participation was voluntary, the swimmers also had to be personally motivated to make the effort and commitment necessary. Overall, it was material evidence and a pleasing realisation for Stephen that the community could conduct itself on a higher plane than what was considered normal or acceptable.

On the negative side, none of the swimmers at the poolside at the start of the session seemed to contemplate the empty pool the same way Stephen did. Once in the pool they seemed technically proficient but lacking grace. The Club and therefore its members were focussed on refining their swimming for the mundane purpose of achieving faster times in order to improve their competitiveness rather than any more profound or heightened experience. The swimmers were continuously directed by the two instructors, who remained fully clothed and outside the pool throughout the session, and never appeared to do anything on their own initiative or as individuals. The community ethos thus prevailed with the primacy of action over inaction, time over timelessness, competitiveness over non-competitiveness, conformity over personal initiative, the group over the individual, and the external over the internal. This all meant to Stephen that there were significant constraints on the Swimming Club as a vehicle for the Power in the community.

Stephen concluded that the positive aspects of the session he had just witnessed were insufficient for the experience of the Power, and key elements of the session were counter to it. However, he had made some encouraging progress in seeing the differences between the public and Swimming Club sessions, and he was still motivated by the realisation of the swimming pool as a reservoir and abode of the Power in the community. He still believed that the future of his mission somehow lay in the swimming pool, and the Swimming Club in particular.

Having finished his coffee and his immediate thoughts on the Swimming Club session, Stephen made his way from the cafe and out of the building. Unfortunately, this time there was no poster, or anything else, to provide him with quick or easy help on what should happen next.

Seventeen

Stephen sat at his bedroom window contemplating his observations of the Swimming Club. He had returned several times to the swimming pool in the evening in order to observe sessions of the Club. Each time he had gone to the poolside café, bought some coffee, then sat at the same seat at the same table as before. He had relaxed, attuned himself to the surroundings, and absorbed everything there was to take in. Each time he had found nothing new of significance to add to his original observations though he had succeeded in confirming to himself that those original observations were correct.

This evening, the date of the next session of the Swimming Club, Stephen had decided to stop going to observe such sessions. His presence and intense interest seemed to have been noticed by some of the participating members of the Club and he was sure he was beginning to be talked about by two or three of them. Such attention risked sabotaging his mission at the swimming pool and, given his lack of further progress, for no apparent gain.

Consequently, Stephen had decided instead to write down his observations in some final form. He had been reluctant to do this before because he feared setting his thoughts down on paper might stop him from keeping a more open and flexible mind on the matter, but there was now little to lose from the exercise. Indeed, he thought there might well be something to gain from now doing so, for he had found in similar circumstances that writing out the various aspects of a dilemma created both a detachment and a different perspective that allowed things to be seen in a new light and thus helped to determine its resolution.

As he had written his observations down, the resolution he had hoped for came about, for when listing his negative observations he had felt compelled to list the positive opposites that would resolve them. The words and phrases he used in this process, as also when listing his positive observations, were in significant part derived from his poem *The Reservoir*. This made him go over the poem with his observations in mind, and where they were correspondingly lacking in some way he used the poem to help complete his new work. When he was finished, he saw that he had written the rough draft of a kind of manual for the Swimming Club members that he thought would help them to realise the Power.

Stephen was initially delighted with this outcome, and was pleased that his poem had served this important purpose, for he saw that just as his poem could not have become what it was without his novel, so his manual could not have become what it was without his poem. Now, however, his delight and pleasure with his manual was replaced with the contemplation of its inherent difficulties, for he was immediately faced with the problem of what to do with it once it was finally complete to his satisfaction. Ideally, it required the active endorsement of the Swimming Club as an organisation, but Stephen knew his manual was completely contrary to the ethos of the Club and had no chance of being accepted. Stephen did not know what, if anything, the Club had in the way of manuals, but he knew that whatever one there was would endorse and promote those very things he had found wanting in his observations of the Club and that his own manual was meant to correct. Stephen would avoid any such existing manual when continuing to write his own to ensure its purity lest it be corrupted in any way by reading a 'bad' one.

The only alternative to the Swimming Club's endorsement Stephen could envisage was to approach its members individually, but he knew this was not at all a realistic prospect either and considerably risky. Given that his manual was as feasible in its rightful domain as *The Fugitive* and *The Reservoir* was in theirs, he could only suppose that it must have a similar role and purpose in progressing his mission, and what that was would be revealed at the appropriate time. In the meantime, he would refine his manual until it was complete.

Eighteen

As Stephen had struggled with the matter of his mission, he had continued with his posting at the depot. He had now been there for about five months and was counting the days to his next posting at a water treatment works on the outskirts of Kirknane. He was working at the swimming pool quite frequently due to the long-term health problems, and thus absences, of the water operative currently posted to the pool. He enjoyed these visits: not only for getting out the depot but for the opportunity to be at the swimming pool. Sometimes, if the timing was right, he got to contemplate the pool when it was empty of swimmers and completely placid. At such times he could best experience the Power latent in the pool.

Today, his twenty second last day at the depot, he received an instruction to go to the swimming pool once again: this time to prepare the diving pool for use. The diving pool was screened off from the rest of the pool hall almost to the point of invisibility. It had lain empty and unused for some considerable time. People using the swimming pool were generally not aware of it. Stephen had not been aware of it whenever he had gone to work on the swimming pool, for the diving pool's deactivated status meant it only required an annual check. He had also not been aware of it when observing the use of the swimming pool.

Stephen did not know why the diving pool had not been used for so long or why it had now to be prepared for use. Were there still people who used it? If so it would surely not have remained empty for so long. He checked the maintenance and repair records - it was, in any case, required by the procedure set down in the water operative's manual for reactivating the pool - but there was no indication of any problem with the pool itself. The records also showed that the pool had not been used for a number of years. This made him even more curious, but he could not ask his supervisor about it, or anyone else in the Water Company for that matter, for fear of coming across as challenging an instruction, so he decided to speak to the staff at the swimming pool to see if they knew anything. If he was sufficiently circumspect about it there should be no repercussions. He went to the reception area at the entrance to the swimming pool building where he found two members of staff standing behind the reception counter.

'Hi there,' said Stephen, addressing both of them simultaneously, 'I've been told to prepare the diving pool for re-use - do you know who's going to use it?'

Stephen tried to sound and look as nonchalant as possible about his question rather than as interested as he really was, and to make the question seem somehow necessary for him carrying out the task, but, feeling nervous at how convincing was his pretence, he took the looks he got in response as one of suspicion.

'I'm just curious,' he quickly added, and then inwardly squirmed at how unconvincing he thought *that* came across.

The two staff members looked at each other and muttered a few words between them before returning to face Stephen.

'No, we don't know,' said one of them. 'I'm surprised it's being re-opened though,' he added, 'nobody used it before. I think that's why it was closed down.'

Disappointed with their response, Stephen thanked them nevertheless and left the reception area. He soon came across two other members of staff one after the other and approached each of them in the same manner as with the staff at reception, but with what he regarded as somewhat more conviction. However, they were equally unaware of who was going to use the diving pool, and thus why it was being re-opened. Stephen decided he had better not ask anyone else but consoled himself with the expectation that eventually the truth would out.

Stephen went to work on the diving pool. After a few checks of the pool and its equipment, he began to fill the pool with water. It was a somewhat slow process, but one that was required to be constantly monitored, so he sat on a bench at the edge of the pool and watched it fill up. As he did so, he became bewitched by the experience as if hypnotised by the slowly rising water. Eventually, the surface of the water reached its proper level and Stephen went and turned off the supply. Returning to the diving pool, with its now completely placid surface in its now silent and peaceful setting, he felt compelled to sit back down on the bench and stare at the pool. As he savoured the sense of profundity, mystery and latent possibility its depth evoked, the presence of the Power was palpable to him. The diving pool was another reservoir in the community! Another abode of the Power! Moreover, the greater depth of the diving pool compared to the swimming pool made contemplating it an even more satisfying experience. To his delight, Stephen realised he had found the means of progressing his mission that he was seeking.

Stephen contemplated what that progress entailed whilst remaining sitting on the bench and looking at the diving pool. It didn't take him long to determine what he should do next. He should write a diving manual for the diving pool just as he had written a swimming manual for the swimming pool. Indeed, he expected it would be in some way based on the swimming manual that, after much refining since his first draft, he now regarded as virtually complete. The swimming manual now revealed its true purpose and practicality, and Stephen again felt vindicated in his conduct. As with that swimming manual, he would avoid any existing diving manual when writing his own to ensure its purity lest it be corrupted in any way by reading a 'bad' one. In order to properly write a diving manual, however, he must now somehow find out about diving.

This was the second time Stephen had been sent to the swimming pool and found a reservoir and abode of the Power - and an unconscious subversion of the community's power. Indeed, his whole time as a water operative seemed to be a succession of auspicious and timeous events and experiences that to him were altogether much too frequent and appropriate to be explained in terms of coincidence or luck. His only concern was that, on his discovery of the swimming pool as a reservoir, the passing staff member had said it made him want to 'dive in' but he had not realised the full meaning of that statement at the time. If he had, he might have progressed immediately to the diving pool and diving. Not only had he wasted time, but he had failed to fully engage with the Power.

Nineteen

After leaving home, Stephen had walked for half an hour before reaching the tenement in which John Gattonside lived. He had acquired the address from the telephone directory. Gattonside's name had been given to him by one of the staff members at the swimming pool: one of those he had spoken to when enquiring about why the diving pool was being re-activated. The staff member recalled - 'if he remembered correctly' (he did) - that Gattonside had been one of the two or three regular users of the diving pool some years ago when the staff member had helped supervise its use, so he might know what was happening with the diving pool now. Fortunately for Stephen, he was approached by the staff member soon after his encounter with the diving pool, so he quickly discovered what to do next to find out about diving in order to write his diving manual. What better than engaging with someone who had actually used the diving pool, and who might also know why it was being re-activated. Stephen appreciated the auspiciousness of having asked the right staff member.

To one side of the common door to the tenement was the door entry system: a metal panel with a two-way speaker grille at head height and a column of buttons underneath - one for each flat, with the name of its occupant to its right. Stephen found 'John Gattonside' and pressed the associated button for a good few seconds. Since pressing the button only activated a buzzer within the flat itself, Stephen did not know whether it had worked or not. An expectant silence ensued for a little while until broken by an unfamiliar, disembodied voice coming from the speaker grille, asking who was there with an inquiring 'Hello?'

Stephen leaned close in to the speaker grille, almost conspiratorially.

'It's me, Stephen Whyte,' he replied.

'Okay, come on up,' the voice responded, followed by a buzzing noise from the lock for the common door indicating that the door was being temporarily unlocked.

Stephen pushed the heavily sprung door open and, leaving it to close itself, went through the hallway to the foot of the common stair and began climbing it. Gattonside lived on the third - topmost - floor.

Stephen had given considerable thought as to how to approach Gattonside about his diving and the diving pool. He couldn't be open about the purpose of his visit, but he didn't want to be deceitful either. In the end he had decided to present himself as a writer undertaking research about diving for a novel he was developing. He assured himself that this was essentially true, for he was indeed a writer undertaking research on diving, on account of developments ensuing from his novel, so that is how he had approached Gattonside when phoning to ask to meet him.

When Stephen finally reached the top floor he found a man standing at the open front door of his flat at the other end of the landing.

'You must be John Gattonside?' he called over to him.

Stephen cringed with embarrassment at the somewhat witless redundancy of his question. He had blurted it out to fill an otherwise awkward silence before reaching where Gattonside stood waiting for him. He was also cringing at his loudness - his voice was nervously pitched higher than normal and amplified further by the stone walls and floor of the landing - and the thought that he had broadcast his presence to the other occupants of the top floor contrary to his quiet and private nature and the somewhat covert nature of his visit.

'Yes, I am John Gattonside,' confirmed the man as Stephen reached him.

'Please come in,' he said, and stood to one side to allow Stephen into the hall of the flat.

'Just go through to the sitting-room,' he added as he closed his front door, then followed Stephen into the sitting room.

'Please take a seat. Would you like a drink?'

'No thanks,' replied Stephen as he sat down.

Gattonside sat down opposite and they exchanged a few more pleasantries before turning to the purpose of the visit.

'So you've come to ask me about diving?'

'Yes. I have to admit, I didn't know there was a group of divers in Kirknane. I've never been a user of the swimming pool though.'

'Well, even if you were a frequent visitor to the swimming pool you might not have been aware of us. We only dived during the weekly sessions of the Swimming and Diving Club.'

'Excuse me, did you say Swimming and *Diving* Club?'

'Yes, that's what it used to be called. Anyway, the swimming pool management wouldn't allow use of the diving pool at any other time because it would mean having to have an extra member of staff to supervise and act as a life guard as the diving pool was cut off from the swimming pool. They didn't think the cost was justified, and to be fair they were probably right, for there would normally only be the two or three of us at any one club session. There might not have been anyone at all at other times.'

'Is that all the divers there were?'

'Unfortunately, that was pretty much the case. There were a few others who showed an interest but there was only the three of us that were in any way serious about it. Then one of the other two died, and some time after that the other one stopped for health reasons before passing away also. That was the end for me as well, for it wasn't the same doing it on my own. Since the diving pool was no longer used at all it was closed down and, with nobody diving, the Kirknane Swimming and Diving Club became simply the Kirknane Swimming Club.'

Stephen now felt that he had reached a point in the conversation, and had established a sufficient rapport, that would allow him to ask Gattonside about his own diving experience.

'As I told you on the phone, I need to get as full an understanding of the diving experience as possible for a novel I am researching. Obviously, this is made a lot harder with no diving taking place any more! The best I can do is speak to someone who used to dive seriously and you seem to be the best - only - person to do that. Could you describe to me your own experience?'

'Certainly. My initial impulse to dive was due in part to a certain bravado as a young man, but also in part to seeing a genuine personal challenge in being able to dive into the diving pool from the heights of the diving platforms just like the divers I had observed. Once I started, however, I quickly appreciated diving for its own sake. At first for the raw, elemental experience of flying through the air into a deep pool of water. Then later, without losing that sense of fundamental exhilaration, for the challenge to develop and perfect my diving in all its aspects including the performance of the more difficult and demanding dives.'

Gattonside then engaged in a long discourse about the different types of dives he had mastered. Though Stephen doubted the value to him of what Gattonside had to say on the matter, he maintained an attentive interest both out of politeness and on the off chance of hearing something useful.

'Anyway,' declared Gattonside, ending his discourse, 'as I gained experience I found the quality of my dive, to me at least, was affected by the quality of my whole conduct, from before ascending the diving platform steps to after exiting the pool after the dive. Because of this I developed my diving into something of a ritual. I had a set starting point at the base of the steps to the diving platforms. Standing there, I would begin by looking at the diving pool and allow myself to be drawn into it, for it had an hypnotic effect on me. This allowed me to compose myself physically and mentally, and then to concentrate on contemplating the possible dives I could perform. I would picture myself executing them till eventually settling on a particular dive. I would then climb the steps in a set way and at a set pace, and with a mindful and purposeful intent. When I reached the particular platform for my dive I would walk to its front edge, or wherever I would begin the dive from, and compose myself again taking account of my new position. I would then picture myself performing the dive. Then I would dive. Once I had entered the water I would maintain my diving posture on entry until I had gone as deep as the momentum from the dive would take me. Then I would give up my diving posture and, relaxing completely, let myself be brought to the surface of the diving pool. Then I would exit the pool in a set manner. Once out of the pool and standing up, I would acknowledge the dive as being completed. And that was that,' Gattonside ended, with a look of evident pride at his accomplishment at diving, and not a little pleasure at Stephen's intent interest at what he had to say - something he was not used to.

Stephen could not help noticing, and taking pleasure in, the way in which Gattonside had related his diving experience. His words had seemed carefully chosen and spoken with a heartfelt sincerity in an almost reverential tone. His description of his diving was unusually articulate compared to the normal speech of Kirknane. He had obviously given thought and consideration to his diving experience. Stephen had been particularly taken by Gattonside describing his diving as being 'something of a ritual' and how that ritual involved contemplating the pool and letting himself be brought to the surface of the water after his dive. He asked Gattonside to elaborate on the latter.

'Once I had entered the water,' Gattonside explained, 'I would surrender myself to the water's elemental forces, for I found this - this may sound a bit weird - somehow profoundly satisfying, for it felt like I was engaging with a greater power - one that wasn't human. It wasn't some added on thrill though. It was an integral part of the whole dive in which each part and aspect mattered and where the whole was more than the sum of its parts.'

Gattonside's response surprised and delighted Stephen for, along with Gattonside's contemplation of the pool at the start of his dives and the pool's hypnotic effect on him, it confirmed he had now found someone else in the community with, at least in some way and to some extent, an experience of the Power. He could now equate his contemplations at the reservoir as mentally diving into the depths of the reservoir with an issue, and passively allowing it to return to the surface with an answer. It was the first time he had experienced such a sense of affinity with another person in Kirknane on anything profounder than some of the mundanities of everyday life.

'Did you share your approach to diving and the experience with the other divers, or anyone else?'

'I did with the other two serious divers, but nobody else. There didn't seem any point as it wouldn't have meant anything to them.'

'What response did you get from the other two divers?'

'Nothing much came of it; it didn't seem to mean anything even to them.'

Stephen went quiet as he absorbed Gattonside's responses to his questions.

'So you're writing a novel?' inquired Gattonside, but more to keep the conversation going than out of genuine interest.

Stephen was somewhat taken aback by the question, and annoyed with himself for not being prepared for it. He was afraid his 'deceit' might be exposed, and that his countenance alone might be sufficient to betray him.

'Yes,' he replied, trying to appear sincere but in a tone suggesting he had nothing to say on the matter, 'but it's quite difficult to explain, especially with so much still to sort out.'

'Oh,' responded Gattonside with his own finality on the subject, generously assuming Stephen's reticence was modesty.

Stephen was embarrassed at his response to the question, for his presence in Gattonside's home was to inquire into a subject that seemed as personal and as close to Gattonside's heart as Stephen's writing was to his. What else could he say, however, without adding to his story about writing a novel that he had already forsaken - a story he had already found difficult to maintain?

'I take it you know that the diving pool has been re-activated?' asked Stephen, ending the awkward moment with a question he intended asking anyway.

'Yes, so I heard.'

'Do you know why?' inquired Stephen, and explained how his interest was due to his work.

'No, it doesn't make sense to me. I can't see anyone using it - at least not in the serious and sustained way that might justify re-opening it.'

'You won't use it yourself?'

'No I won't, I'm a little too old and out of condition, but even if I did try to take up diving again, the pool would be closed before I was fit enough! I just can't see it staying open that long. To me it belongs to another era.'

'No-one's approached you to coach or anything else like that, seeing as you're the only diver in Kirknane?'

'No, I'm not involved and haven't been asked to get involved.'

Stephen went quiet again, offering no further questions, so Gattonside then offered him an old amateur ciné film, taken by one of the other divers, that showed Gattonside diving. He had got it out in anticipation of Stephen's visit. He told Stephen he could keep it as he could no longer play it himself for lack of the right equipment. Stephen was delighted to have the film - he still had an old projector and screen, that had belonged to his parents, that would allow him to watch it - though it made him feel even more embarrassed at the meanness of his reticence over speaking about his novel.

Thereafter returning to pleasantries, the visit came to a natural end. Leaving Gattonside's flat with some final words of thanks and departure, Stephen made his way home tremendously pleased with the success of his visit, for he had got out of it so much of what he had hoped for.

Twenty

Once he was back home from his meeting with John Gattonside, Stephen went into the roof space of his flat and retrieved his parents' ciné film projector and screen – he duly noted the auspicious circumstance of having the equipment necessary to screen Gattonside's film. He took it into his sitting room and set it all up. He had the projector sitting on his coffee table and the self-standing screen facing it at a distance of about three metres. He loaded the film onto the projector and began playing it. To his relief, though it had not been used for some years and had been gathering dust in his roof space, the projector worked fine.

Stephen carefully watched the film, which only lasted for a few minutes, several times over. The film showed Gattonside performing a dive from just before the start of his ritual until just after the end of it. To Stephen, the whole performance of the dive conformed to how Gattonside had described it to him. He was pleased with what he saw, for it helped him to appreciate what Gattonside had said, and reinforced his belief that he had found at least part of what he was looking for: a way for others to experience in the community what he had experienced at the reservoir. A tired Stephen went to bed deeply satisfied about how things were going with his mission.

The following morning, however, Stephen had a very different mood, for he now had to face up to something that he had previously put to the back of his mind because he was keen to stay positive about his engagement with diving. He had to admit that, whatever the actual or potential merits of the diving experience, only a handful of people had participated in it seriously in the past and it was unlikely to attract even that level of participation now. Society had changed since the diving pool had closed; people had generally become less active and less interested in fringe pursuits like diving as if such things now belonged to a different era - as Gattonside himself had said.

Moreover, Gattonside's diving experience appeared not to have had any profound effect on the rest of his life. He was seemingly still a conventional member of the community in a way Stephen was not and could not be. Stephen thought that if he had found someone fundamentally like himself, such a person would be as alienated from the rest of the community as he was. Instead, Gattonside had given up diving when he was the only serious diver left because 'it wasn't the same doing it on his own.' Furthermore, his heightened articulation of his diving experience seemed restricted to that description alone. The rest of his speaking was as mundane as that of any other person in Kirknane.

Nonetheless, Stephen's discovery of Gattonside's diving experience was his only success so far in what had already been a long and difficult mission. More than that, there was still his diving manual. Given that his previous writings had all served as stepping stones in his mission, he was confident that the diving manual could perform the same role. Indeed, given the impracticalities and unlikelihood of diving being the means he sought for the community to experience the Power, he believed that was almost certainly the diving manual's purpose. He must therefore continue with his writing of it and be guided by inspiration.

To that end, Stephen sensed that Gattonside's film had something significant yet to contribute. Fortunately, he had taken the day off in anticipation of his meeting with Gattonside in order to give him time immediately afterwards to absorb and consider what was said without the hindrance of work, so he was free to continue watching the film and see what transpired.

Through the day, therefore, Stephen continued to view the film every once in a while and think about it between each viewing. Each time he replayed the film he looked at the screen with a deliberate air of expectation hoping somehow to induce what he was seeking - but nothing happened. Then he realised he was trying too hard and not allowing the answer to emerge. He therefore relaxed himself absorbing the silence and peacefulness of his flat. Once he was properly attuned to his situation he replayed the film. This time, though the film finished once more without suggesting anything new, he remained in his contemplative state. The fact of the film ending without any progress being made, and him staring at the now blank screen, made him think what might, or should, be on the screen to progress his mission. To Stephen, this sense of possibility and expectation gave the screen an alluring, profound and mysterious depth. Then he realised he was contemplating the screen as a reservoir! An abode of the Power!

Stephen was delighted, for he quickly appreciated that the film screen was not only the reservoir of the most popular cultural form in Kirknane, but one which viewers must sit in front of and contemplate for a considerable period of time. It also meant that the power of the community had been subverted much further than by the swimming and diving pools alone, albeit again unconsciously.

To Stephen, without him even actually writing it, the diving manual had served its purpose. It had led him to Gattonside and his film, and thus to the reservoir that he knew was the one he had been seeking. His fatalism and belief in his mission was once again vindicated.

Twenty One

Every reservoir, and thus abode of the Power, that Stephen had encountered had inspired a new writing directly related to it: the reservoir in the hills had inspired his poem *The Reservoir*, the reservoir as the swimming pool had inspired his swimming manual, and the reservoir as the diving pool had inspired his diving manual. Having now encountered the reservoir as film screen, he expected to be inspired to write a screenplay for a film. This inspiration failed to materialise however. His expectation disappointed, he concluded that he was either not yet at the stage of writing a screenplay or wasn't in fact meant to write one, and that he must therefore start from a different position. What that position was he was not that sure, so he thought he should best start from the most basic and 'earliest' starting point he could think of so as not to miss anything. He determined that that starting point would be to attend the cinema in Kirknane. It was something he thought he should do in any case in order to better understand cinema, and in Kirknane in particular, for his only experience of going to the cinema was in childhood. As an adult, he had no more inclination to watch a contemporary film than he had to read a contemporary book, although he couldn't help absorbing a certain awareness and knowledge of contemporary cinema in the course of his day to day life in Kirknane. This was generally by passively listening to others talking about it, or reading film reviews in the Kirknane Advertiser for want of something to read. Thus needing the experience, and thinking that perhaps his lack of such experience was the cause of his lack of inspiration, Stephen was going to the cinema.

Almost immediately on entering the foyer of the multiplex cinema, Stephen was conscious of being on his own, for everyone else there seemed to be with someone else. Aloneness was looked on somewhat suspiciously in Kirknane, for it suggested someone unable or unwilling to participate fully in the social ethos of the community. Of course people were often on their own out of necessity, but this was usually due to circumstances of work or travel and understood accordingly, but at somewhere like a cinema the fact of being alone would be seen as one of choice or social failure, so Stephen felt a little uncomfortable at waiting on his own in a line to buy a ticket for the film he was about to watch.

It took only a few minutes for him to reach the front of the line and buy his ticket. There were several films to choose from but none that particularly appealed to him. Films were considered a vital and integral part of life in Kirknane and he thus expected them to embody and promote the community ethos that he found so much fault with. This was why it was the first time he had been to the cinema since childhood – he believed he last went when he was about ten years old. The film that he decided to watch was the most popular of the moment. He thought that to observe the cinema in the community - the purpose of his visit, and the first with the awareness and intent he now had - the most popular film would be the best to watch as its popularity suggested it would be most in tune with the community. The potential of this popularity in regard to his mission, in contrast to diving or even swimming, excited him.

After getting his ticket, Stephen went straight to the particular cinema that his film was being shown at without, as others were doing, stopping to buy something to eat or drink for when watching the film. He offered his ticket to the person controlling admission to the cinema. The person checked it and tore a part of it off, so it couldn't be used again, before returning it to Stephen.

When Stephen entered the cinema there was already a handful of people there who had gone in before him. He was surprised at this, for he had made a point of being considerably early so as to observe as much as possible - to miss nothing - of the community's cinema-going experience, and had therefore expected to be the first person there. He chose a seat roughly in the centre of the auditorium especially for being in the midst of the audience so as to better observe everything. He would otherwise have instinctively chosen somewhere less conspicuous on the fringe of the seating and towards the back.

After a while of nothing much happening, he looked at his watch: there was about ten minutes before the film was due to start. As if prompted by his checking of the time, a small but steady stream of people began entering the cinema and choosing their seats. As the place filled up, the new arrivals came to sit increasingly closer to him and the noise level inside the cinema rose steadily. By the time the film was due to start, the cinema was almost full. Stephen was hemmed in on either side, and otherwise completely surrounded by other people, and at the same time engulfed by the noise and chatter of the audience near and far. This was as he had anticipated, but it still made him feel very uncomfortable with him being unaccustomed and disinclined to such an experience.

At last the cinema lights went out for the screening of the film and, in the anonymity of the dark, Stephen immediately felt more at ease. The audience went quiet in their anticipation of the film starting. Stephen consciously emptied his mind of any preconceptions of films and cinema-going, and settled back into his seat to watch the film. The sudden appearance of light and sound palpably grabbed the attention of the audience, and continued to hold that attention as the light and sound changed constantly thereafter.

Stephen found the film very well made for its kind, so he could understand its popularity, but he also found that popularity worrying given some of the film's content. He often found himself laughing at the comedy in the film along with the rest of the audience, but there were times when he found the comedy too crude to be funny. He also found some of the violence difficult to watch and its most extreme parts simply disturbing - especially with the idea that it was meant, and enjoyed, as entertainment. There were explicit sex scenes that he found dismayingly coarse, and accompanied by equally coarse language that also peppered the rest of the film. He also found the storyline somewhat contrived and superficial, as if it was more a vehicle for the comedy, sex and violence of the film than important in itself.

As for the audience, there were occasional verbal outbursts that pierced the soundtrack at its quieter moments. These outbursts often involved crude language or expressions of approval of those very aspects that Stephen disapproved of the most, or both together. Moreover, some of the people immediately surrounding him were eating, drinking and speaking to each other so noisily and sometimes animatedly – albeit about the film - that he couldn't help being distracted by it to some extent. This all seemed to be treated as normal: there was no protest of any kind from either the cinema staff or from others in the audience. To Stephen, the content of the film and the behaviour of the audience reflected the social and cultural mores of the community and the parallels with the public session of the swimming pool were immediately obvious.

Nonetheless, Stephen had also found some positive aspects to his cinema experience. There was the kinship of a shared cultural experience. This was something he had not experienced in Kirknane as an adult at least. There was also the elemental aspect of sitting in the dark and watching the changing light on the screen, and how that changing light, along with the changing sound of the film's soundtrack, enthralled and affected the audience. Those few faces he contrived, and was able, to see seemed to have the same rapt gaze that he had at his favourite place at the reservoir when contemplating the scene before him. Neither the film nor the audience had been equal to the occasion, but it nonetheless reinforced the potential to Stephen of the screen as a reservoir, as an abode of the Power.

At the end of the film, the lights immediately came on and everyone began streaming out of the cinema animatedly talking to each other: about the film judging by what Stephen could hear. He would have liked to remain in his seat to think some more about what he had just experienced, but as he was sitting in the centre of the cinema with the lights fully on he would have been too self-consciously in the public eye to contemplate properly. Nevertheless, he had done what he had come to do, so he left with that satisfaction in mind as he joined the mass exit.

Twenty Two

In order to be able to attend its meetings in pursuit of his mission, Stephen had joined the Kirknane Film Club and paid the annual membership fee. A week or so ago he had received his membership card in the post along with various written material about the club and its activities. Thus able to attend the next of its monthly meetings, he now made his way to the cinema for that very purpose.

The Film Club usually held its monthly meetings at Cinema 5 of the cinema multiplex. Though the smallest of the cinemas there, it was big enough to accommodate the usual turnout for club meetings and the intimate atmosphere afforded by its size was conducive to the discussions that took place. Each meeting was usually organised around the screening of a particular 'classic' film that was not otherwise normally available for viewing but was considered worthy in some way of such a re-screening. The screening was then followed by a discussion between club members about the film. Sometimes someone who was involved in the making of the film being screened, such as a writer, actor, director or producer, made an appearance and took part in the proceedings, and this usually included a question and answer session with all the club members that were present.

Stephen approached the Film Club meeting he was attending, including the film screening, with somewhat more enthusiasm than his earlier attendance at a public screening. Just as he had found his experience of the public screening to be akin to the public sessions of the swimming pool, both in terms of the conduct of those involved and the qualities of the experience as seen by him, so he expected the experience of the Film Club meeting to be at least akin to the Swimming Club sessions - though he would put that preconception to one side when making his observations. His enthusiasm was moderated, however, by the knowledge that he would be considerably more conspicuous attending a club meeting compared to a public screening. Everyone else would know each other to some extent whereas he would be the newcomer and noticed as such - there would be no 'neutral' café to observe from. He knew just how uncomfortable such an appearance could be for him with it being so counter to his innate character. Nevertheless, his sense of mission gave him the determination to attend.

At last Stephen reached the entrance to the cinema building. He hesitated a little at this point for his anxiety about his attending the meeting had a last minute resurgence. He had to pause and remind himself of the benefits, indeed the necessity, of him going inside and attending. His resolve sufficiently reinforced, he made his way into the building.

As he reached Cinema 5 he again became somewhat anxious, and was not helped by the contrast with the other people about him who were also attending the club meeting, who were seemingly care-free and enthusiastic. When he entered Cinema 5 he found that the others present were gathered close together towards the front of the seating. He noticed, however, that some people were scattered a little apart and aback from the main body of attendees. He took this as allowing him to do likewise so he sat down on his own, but close enough to everyone else that he could not be seen as in some way rejecting being part of the others as a group. As he surveyed the scene before him, he saw that there were one or two other people who were also there on their own. It was only then that it dawned on him that the specialised nature of the club allowed people to attend on their own without the negative associations such behaviour commonly attracted in Kirknane. This was unlike the situation with public screenings. He also realised that, in comparison to the Swimming Club, the cinema seats being fixed and facing forwards made it much harder, and thus much less likely, for him to be noticed and observed by all those in front of him. He felt much more comfortable at the situation he found himself in compared to the one he had nervously anticipated. Indeed, he now saw that it was his very nervousness about attending that had blinded him to any mitigating factors. Nevertheless, he still felt somewhat conspicuous being here for the first time amongst people who must be at least familiar to each other, and he noticed the odd inquisitive glance and what looked like muttering about a 'new member.'

Stephen had not come early in order to observe as much as possible, as he had with the public screening, for he had found the idea too forbidding, so when the convenor of the meeting stood up at the front to welcome everyone and begin the proceedings, Stephen had only been sitting there for a few minutes. The convenor made a few brief club announcements. He then introduced the film to be screened before declaring that, although a discussion about the film would be held immediately after the screening as usual, there was no special guest at this meeting and therefore the discussion would not be guided in that regard. He then gave the signal to the cinema projectionist - who was looking out for it from his eyrie in the projection room at the back of the cinema - to begin the screening. (The idea of the projectionist in his 'eyrie', enclosed on three sides by the projection room, and looking at the cinema from the openness in front of him, made Stephen think of himself in his shelter looking at the reservoir). Everyone looked to the screen in anticipation and Stephen pleasantly sensed the audience's mood - just as he had done so at the public screening. A few moments later, the lights went down and, after a brief period of darkness and silent expectation from the audience, the film began by bursting out in light and noise.

From what Stephen understood from the convenor's introduction, the film was a romantic comedy and had been chosen for the quality of its writing and social observation. As he began to watch it, he emptied any such considerations, that to him were preconceptions, from his mind in order to form unbiased impressions of the film.

Stephen was pleasantly surprised to find the film quite entertaining and well written, and with good social observation. Taking into account the difference in genre between the two films he had now seen, there was a good deal less of the coarser elements in the film at the club screening than the one he had watched at the public one, and the story line was more substantial and plausible. He wondered if this was also due to the club film having been made some twenty years ago and whether such a film would be made today.

As with the conduct of, and contrast between, the Swimming Club members and the public swimming session users, to Stephen the Film Club members were certainly better behaved and seemed more serious than the public cinemagoers. In particular, there were no verbal outbursts, with or without coarse language, and it appeared that no-one around him had brought food or drink into the cinema or, if they had, they had consumed it quietly and unobtrusively. This made the experience more like him contemplating the reservoir than the public screening had.

The positive aspects that Stephen found at the public screening he also found repeated here: the sense of kinship of a shared cultural experience, the elemental aspects of the changing light on the screen in the otherwise dark cinema, the enthrallment of the audience with the changing light, and their rapt gaze reminiscent of his own while contemplating the reservoir – it seemed to Stephen that the Film Club audience held their gaze even more consistently than the public audience. Moreover, this was all enhanced by the better behaviour of the club members.

When the film ended, the lights came back up and the convenor stood up and faced the attendees in order to initiate and moderate the discussion of the film. Stephen was intent on following the discussion closely, for the nature and quality of the discussion was a vital element for him in understanding the nature and quality of the community's engagement with film, and thus the appropriate approach for his mission - especially since the Film Club members were the people in the community he believed would be the most receptive to his efforts. He was also keen to hear anything that indicated any differences in how the film was regarded between when the film was made and its screening now. This might give him some perspective on how film had developed in the community in that period; a period which was half the lifetime to date of what he saw as Kirknane's present distinctive manifestation.

Stephen found the discussion, though at times animated, was conducted in a serious and disciplined manner. Indeed, the Film Club members talked about the film in a way he had never heard people talk about books. There was a palpable sense, as with the Swimming Club, of a common, shared purpose. He also found, however, that the conduct of the Film Club members in their discussion had similar failings to the conduct of the Swimming Club members in the swimming pool: there was external direction, but this time by the convenor; there was external validation, but now provided by other speakers; there was an emphasis on technical aspects of the film's production - and at the same time there was no mention of the way the film was lit even though there was an obvious difference to Stephen in the lighting of the two films he had now seen; and there was competitiveness between the participants in the way people seemed to be scoring debating points. Stephen was also disappointed that nothing emerged from the debate that related to the difference in time between when the two films he had now watched had been made. Nonetheless, the Film Club did have a debate whereas there was no debate at the Swimming Club in regard to their session. Instead, the two swimming instructors had simply spoken to the swimmers about their performance without any response from them other than an acknowledgement of what they were being told.

As with the members of the Swimming Club, Stephen found that the engagement of the members of the Film Club was not sufficiently of the higher nature he was seeking although in both cases it was markedly better than that of the general public. Their seriousness seemed misdirected and lacking any sense of profundity. Indeed, some of the members taking part in the discussion about the film seemed taken up with what he saw as trivial aspects. He also heard nothing that suggested a thought or opinion in any way counter to the social and cultural norms of the community in the way he was hoping. Nonetheless, the film was sufficiently well made that he could see film could be like poetry in its ability to condense something complex both concisely and sublimely, and could be like a novel in its ability to tell a story. Moreover, the members of the Film Club clearly had the potential to be his desired audience.

Eventually, the discussion having faded somewhat, the convenor brought the meeting to an end. Everyone made their way from the cinema with many in animated conversation as they picked over the scraps of the discussion. Stephen joined in the mass exit, glad that he had attended. He would go home and fully absorb and reflect on his cinema experiences to date, and then proceed from there.

Twenty Three

As with the cinema, Stephen had not visited Kirknane library for some years until now compelled to do so for the sake of his mission. Having contemplated his experience of the Film Club meeting that he had attended, he had become more positive about its potential. He was now focussed on how the club members had shown in their meeting that they took film seriously and had the potential to be changed by it. He reasoned that if he could find a film that could evoke the Power, get it screened at a meeting of the Film Club, and discussed afterwards with him as moderator providing the necessary guidance, the result could be a fulfilment of his mission. It would not be a contemporary film, for contemporary cinema appeared to be little better than contemporary literature. However, it seemed that cinemagoers, of the Film Club at least, did not reject the older cinema of Kirknane in the way that the older literature was rejected by contemporary readers, although it was treated with some suspicion. Stephen thought that there might be a film from the older cinema that could serve his purpose and yet be acceptable enough to the Film Club that it would be allowed to be screened. Given the special regard the community of Kirknane gave to its own films, and a certain concomitant antipathy towards films made elsewhere, he knew the film he was seeking must be one made in Kirknane to have a realistic chance of succeeding.

Stephen, therefore, was going to the library to see if he could find some kind of guide to, or history of, Kirknane films that gave enough appropriate treatment of each film that he could properly assess them for his purpose. He didn't know the genre or any other specific aspect of the film he was looking for, other than its ability to evoke the Power, but he was certain he would know he had found it if he came across it.

Once inside the library, Stephen quickly surveyed the place. It looked remarkably similar to the last time he had been there, despite being so long ago. Although a writer and a keen reader, he did not frequent the library as it didn't stock the books he liked to read. He also found the library an unwelcoming and unpleasant environment: the seating was very public rather than secluded, it was all brightly lit with neon lights, and it was often distractingly noisy. In all, it was counter to his sensibility, for it was a sensibility that preferred a secluded corner with subtle lighting. It did accord, however, with the sensibility of the community as a whole by stocking the books and other material that reflected its tastes and preferences, and in an acceptable environment, i.e., as a place conducive to social intercourse.

Stephen made his way to the film section of the library. There was a considerable selection that reflected the primacy of film in the community's culture. He browsed through the books by reading their titles on the spine, with his head leaning to one side almost at a right angle to his body. The title alone was usually sufficient to decide if a book was the one he was looking for, though he occasionally had to pull one out and have a closer look.

Then, at last, he came across a large-sized book entitled *A History of Kirknane Cinema: A Film by Film Guide*. As soon as he read the title, he thought he had found the book he was looking for. He took the book from the shelf and leafed through it. He was delighted to confirm it was, indeed, the very thing he sought. Each film had its own substantial entry comprising in turn: a detailed description of the key elements of the film itself, some stills from the film, some explanatory comments and observations made about the film by some of the leading people involved in the making of it, and an in-depth critical assessment by the author of the book - the film critic for the Kirknane Advertiser. If the film he was looking for existed, he would find it in this book.

Stephen stayed in the library all day, taking occasional breaks, as he made his way through the book. The staff eyed him somewhat curiously, for not only had they never seen him in there before but he was spending all day there, and in a seemingly slightly strange manner.

His search did not go well, as each film he read about failed to be the one he was looking for and reduced the number of possible films that were left. His initially eager and hopeful mood became increasingly desperate and pessimistic.

Eventually he finished the book. The film was not there. He was left terribly disappointed and with no immediate idea of what to do next.

Twenty Four

Stephen's posting at the depot was coming to an end when he was sent to the swimming pool for what would be the last time. His task was to de-activate the diving pool. This was perplexing to Stephen for it was only a short while ago that he had re-activated it. From what he could gather from talking to the swimming pool staff – as guardedly as possible – no effort whatsoever had been made to encourage people to use it, and the staff had received no instruction to promote even any awareness of the fact of it being available to use. It had remained as ignored as before.

Despite this final task, the failure of his mission in regard to his fellow water operatives, and him not enjoying being in the depot office for it being the very antithesis of his preferred working conditions in various critical aspects, Stephen's time at the depot had nonetheless been vital and highly valuable to his mission. His work visits to the swimming pool had not only let him discover reservoirs, and thus abodes of the Power, in Kirknane, but they had softened considerably his leaving the reservoir and returning to the community and his place in it.

His next posting, for the usual six months, would be at Kirknane's water treatment works. It was here that the harmful condition of the community's waste water was mitigated as much as possible through various treatments before leaving the community and returning – released - to nature.

What effect this new posting would have on his mission he could not yet tell, but he had begun to have an uncomfortable feeling that it somehow didn't matter, that the failure to find a suitable film as a vehicle for his mission was not only his lowest point so far, but marked the end – or at least the beginning of the end - of that mission.

Moreover, the social engagement that he had undertaken and endured for the sake of his mission had been an increasing strain on his very private minded character and reclusive nature. He didn't know how much longer he could sustain his efforts to overcome that character and nature, and worried about its effects. He feared a self-destruction as a means of escape or release, for it was something he had done in the past when a situation had become too much for him.

Twenty Five

Stephen was sitting outside - just in front of his shelter - basking in the dawn. It was a bright, dry and clear day with the wonderful sharpness of the early hours of such a morning. However, as he enjoyed taking it all in, he heard the barely audible noise of what sounded to him like a vehicle engine. Straining to hear better, he thought it must be a truck and that it was at the other end of the reservoir at the one part out of view from where he was. There was a rough track that ended at the reservoir there, that connected with the road to the works, so it was possible for a truck to be there. However, no-one came to the reservoir normally and if someone did, the incumbent operative was supposed to be informed beforehand and reported to on arrival - neither of which had happened to Stephen in this instance.

Feeling compelled to investigate immediately, Stephen set off towards where the noise was coming from. As he approached, he could hear the sound of the engine ever more clearly, becoming certain it was the same noise the water company tank trucks made when their engines were being used for pumping out the contents of their tanks.

When he reached the bend in the reservoir after which he might be seen, he concealed his approach.

Finally reaching where the track from the road to the works ended at the reservoir, and remaining hidden, he could now see there was indeed a water company tank truck there. With the truck having been reversed into position, the back of it - and therefore the back of its tank - was only a metre or so from the water's edge. A flexible pipe led from the back of the tank and ended submerged in the reservoir. Stephen thought it must be in quite deep - he knew the water was deep there - for despite the vigour of the engine in its role as a pump, the surface of the water was almost completely undisturbed. Stephen recognised the lone water operative who was sitting at the wheel of the truck and seemingly reading a paper. Of all the operatives he had tried to engage with in pursuit of his mission while at the depot, he was the one Stephen had had the least success with. Indeed he had been somewhat hostile to Stephen, and at the same time ingratiatingly friendly toward the depot management.

Stephen was mystified as to what was being discharged into the reservoir, and disturbed by the secretive manner in which it was being done. As he continued to observe what was going on, he went over in his mind the factors that troubled him: he hadn't been informed of this operation as he should have been; it was being carried out much earlier than normal working hours at a time when he would be expected to be in his bed; and it was being done at the one part of the reservoir out of sight, and out of normal earshot, of the works and his accommodation instead of at the works itself where all such discharging was supposed to be carried out. Moreover, of all the operatives who could be undertaking the task, it was the one most favourable towards the water company management and the least favourable towards himself, so approaching - confronting - him would be particularly difficult.

Eventually, the truck was finished with its discharging, and the change in the engine noise when it had finished pumping alerted the operative. Immediately getting out the driver's cab, he retrieved the pipe from the reservoir, coiled it, then fixed it to the back of the truck's tank where it was normally kept. Returning to the driver's cab, he then drove away - Stephen presumed back to Kirknane.

Once the truck was out of sight, Stephen emerged from hiding and went over to where the truck had stood. There was scarcely any sign of it having been there - the dry, stony track and surrounding ground barely showing anything in the way of tyre marks or other disturbance - and even then only noticeable if closely looked for. Stephen looked in to the water: there was nothing that suggested something had just been discharged into the reservoir there. If he had not been outside that early and did not have such acute hearing, he would almost certainly not have known anything of what had happened here.

Stephen then made his way back to the works to get a water testing kit and returned with it to where the discharge had taken place; he wanted to take samples of the water there before the discharge was further diluted. Having taken the samples, he returned to the works where he put them through various tests that were done routinely at the reservoir. The test results showed nothing wrong with the water quality and gave no indication that something had been added to the water. Stephen then tried other tests that were only conducted in abnormal or emergency situations. The results of these tests revealed strong concentrations of certain chemicals that should not be present in the water. Stephen consulted the hazard reference books that were kept at the reservoir for such circumstances: to his alarm they described the chemicals as combining to have the properties of a psychotropic drug.

Stephen also took water samples at the works itself, as it was the part of the reservoir furthest away from where the discharge took place, and put them through the same tests. The results showed the presence of the same psychotropic-forming chemicals but in much lesser concentrations than where the truck had discharged its contents and, according to the hazard reference books, insufficient to materially affect the water supply. However, Stephen thought it was too soon for the discharge he had witnessed earlier to have reached that far, so the traces at the works must have been from an earlier discharge. How many discharges there had already been, and over what timescale, he simply didn't – and couldn't – know; such secret operations, by their very nature, would not be recorded in the log book of visits to the reservoir. He checked the log book nonetheless but, as he expected, there was no indication of such visits.

Over the next few days, Stephen repeated the tests by regularly taking samples from the same two locations. The results indicated the concentrations of the chemicals had progressively equalised across the entire reservoir - the entire water supply of Kirknane - but to a level that was hazardous to human consumption.

Stephen now had to decide what to do about what he knew. According to company procedures he should report it all to the Water Company immediately, but it was a Water Company truck and operative that had carried out the operation and he knew from his time at the depot that they could not have been used without the knowledge and consent of at least one person in charge there. The person he should report the incident to could be that same person. Even if it was someone else, the information would have to be shared with others in order to deal with the matter, and would no doubt soon spread to become common knowledge at the depot. Those responsible for the discharge would thus be alerted to Stephen's awareness of what they had done. This would allow them to take whatever counter measures they deemed necessary. As yet, Stephen didn't know the scale of what was going on, or the reason for it, and therefore how far those responsible might go in dealing with him, but he knew how brutal such agents of the power of the community could be. In his isolation at the reservoir he sensed his vulnerability to what their response might be.

Twenty Six

When Stephen first woke up, so vivid and memorable was his dream that he wondered whether he *had* in fact been dreaming or going over in his mind things that were real. He tried to recall from his time at the reservoir if there was indeed a track at the other end from where his shelter was, and whether a tank truck had come to discharge its load there in circumstances similar to those he had dreamt. He also tried to recall, from both his time while training and at the depot, his real-life experiences of the water operative that was in his dream in case they might provide further evidence of that operative's complicity. Once completely awake, however, Stephen knew he had been dreaming.

Nevertheless, remembering the dream so vividly gave it significance for him, for he hardly ever remembered his dreams so well. Indeed, he felt a strong, instinctive attachment to the story he had dreamt, and a perception that it had meaning not only for himself but for the community of Kirknane as well, and all despite him waking up before the dream had finished. He therefore wrote down what he had just dreamt while it was still fresh in his mind.

When he finished he realised what he had done: he had written the start of a screenplay! Then the dream's significance dawned on him: he had dreamed the film he hadn't been able to find; he had made and watched it in his head! Even the phrase *Poisoned Chalice*, which had memorably but somewhat mysteriously come to him in the course of his dream, now made sense as the title of the film, and one that seemed to him so appropriate in a number of ways. Once again in his mission, a seeming dead-end had been transformed into a new way forward and provided a renewed sense of hope and possibility!

Thus inspired and enthused, Stephen added to and developed what he had written down until he had a rough outline of pretty much the whole film.

Despite his pleasure at what had transpired, Stephen's experience to date tempered his sense of renewed hope and possibility with the expectation of encountering difficulties. As he contemplated what to do next those difficulties soon manifested themselves. Though he now had the film he sought, it was yet to be made rather than the existing 'classic' he had been looking for. What he should do next would be to complete the screenplay and submit it to the Kirknane Film Company, Kirknane's sole film producers. He expected, though, that if he did so, his screenplay would be rejected for much the same reasons his novel had been rejected by Blackburns the publishers. He didn't even have an intuitive sense that submitting his screenplay and having it rejected would somehow progress his mission, unlike his earlier experience of submitting work. Moreover, even if he could somehow find the means to make the film himself, he had no skills or experience in making films and was wholly unsuited constitutionally to the collaborative processes normally involved. He also knew that *Poisoned Chalice* could only work as a film.

However, he recalled reading somewhere quite recently that the government had launched a scheme for aspiring film makers to make their own short films, with technical support available as and when it was wanted. The idea was to allow the aspiring film-makers to make films that would not otherwise get made and to develop their skills and experience at the same time. His lack of skills and experience would thus actually count in his favour in this scheme, and a shorter, simpler film would reduce the involvement of others and therefore the degree of collaboration required. He supposed that if he was somewhat disingenuous about the true nature of the film he wanted to make, he might just get his film approved for the scheme. Whatever his chances truly were, he thought it was the only realistic opportunity to get his film made.

Like any such government scheme, the information available about it would be in Kirknane library, so he wasted no time in getting washed, dressed, and having some breakfast, before leaving for there.

Twenty Seven

When Stephen arrived at the library and entered the building, the same staff were there as at his earlier visit. Moreover, judging by the looks they gave him, it seemed to Stephen as if they recognised him also and recalled his somewhat unusual behaviour. He felt his face flush at a mixture of self-consciousness and guilt. He entertained the thought that part of their job was to identify for the authorities anyone using the library's resources for subversive purposes. He assured himself that he was just being somewhat paranoid because his coming to the library had indeed an essentially subversive purpose. He decided, nevertheless, to avoid exchanging looks with the staff during his visit lest such behaviour, and his expression when doing so, aroused suspicion.

He went to the part of the open plan library where the information he sought was normally located, and searched for what he had come for. Eventually, after not too much effort, he found the information on the new short film scheme. In a folder were a number of copies of an explanatory leaflet and a number of copies of the application form for the scheme. He took out one of the leaflets and one of the application forms. Then he sat down on a nearby seat, put the application form to one side, and began reading the explanatory leaflet.

There was little of substance to the leaflet, as was usually the case with such things, but there was something vital in it that Stephen had not anticipated: criteria for the kind of films that were being sought – he had expected the scheme to be open to any kind of film and thus enhance the chances of getting his film approved. As he read the criteria his heart sank. The scheme administrators were seeking proposals that 'celebrate, honour, and uphold the life of the community and its values.' He realised immediately that the film he had dreamt and now wanted to make would not be accepted with that criteria regardless of any other consideration. To a disgusted and vexed Stephen, the scheme administrators were actually worse than the film company, for their criteria showed they were even more ideologically driven, and their effect on the community would therefore likely be all the more corrosive. He made his way out the library trying to hide his anger and frustration, but realising he still held the leaflet in one hand, and without hardly pausing, he despatched it dismissively and somewhat theatrically into a litter bin.

Twenty Eight

When Stephen got home from the library, he made himself some coffee then went and sat at his bedroom window. He stared out the window towards where the reservoir lay in the hills beyond, and wished more than ever that he was back there.

After a while, his thoughts turned to speculation on what a version of *Poisoned Chalice* that would actually get made would probably be like. He could easily picture aspects of such a film. It would be a thriller with plenty of violent action. A community would be in danger – under attack - from a poisoned water supply, but those responsible would not be from the community itself, far less in positions of authority, but from outside it, and their motivation would involve some kind of rejection of the community's values. Perhaps instead, thought Stephen, the means of attack would be to sabotage the reservoir's dam to unleash a destructive flood on the community - the community lying downriver of the dam and in the same valley. Though he couldn't immediately think what the motivation would be for such an act it would make for a more spectacular film. In any case, the plots of such films were driven by action rather than a cohesive and plausible narrative. The hero would be a handsome, distinguished ex-military or police figure who would use his skills, knowledge and experience - including of the application of violence - to combat and foil the malefactors. There would be a beautiful female lead who would romantically and sexually engage with the hero. There would also be a dramatic culmination to the film where the hero prevailed in protecting the community and upholding its virtues, and a denouement suggesting a romantic future together of the hero and female lead. Although a few folk might quibble with certain relatively minor aspects of such a film, like the degree of explicitness of the sex or violence portrayed, it would have the approval of the community of Kirknane and attract a large audience. It would not, though, encourage critical thinking of Kirknane as a society, or self-questioning by its individual citizens of their life in that society, and thus the two kinds of self-examination that Stephen thought Kirknane vitally required and could be provided through the community's realisation of, and engagement with, the Power. Instead, such a film, in its role as a work of propaganda, would simply help sustain the corrosive nature of Kirknane's existing condition for its people as individuals and as a community.

Stephen's contemplation of the negatives of a *Poisoned Chalice* that would actually get made led to more disturbing thoughts about the cultural condition of Kirknane and his place in regard to it. In his reading of the older literature in its original form, and in his writing in the way of that older literature, was he the last of such a kind just as John Gattonside was the last diver? With cinema displacing literature as the dominant cultural form to an increasing degree, and film-making a collaborative social process, was he as a type of artist the last of such a kind also?

If so, the words that he alone read and used that were specific to the older literature, and the way those words were used, would disappear completely from Kirknane on his demise, and the simpler words and their use favoured by the community would not - could not - replace them in anything other than a mundane and utilitarian sense. The type of artist that he represented would also disappear. The community's ability to articulate a higher intelligence and sensibility would be lost, and that intelligence and sensibility with it. The subtle and sublime life of the Power would have no home, mentally or physically, in Kirknane. The light of old that Stephen lived in, and was trying to convert the community to, would be extinguished.

Whither the Power after that?

More immediately, what then of his mission, and of his faith in the rightness of what he had done and what had happened to him from the day he first started writing?

Twenty Nine

Stephen was sitting at his bedroom window and looking outside, but without really taking anything in, for he was caught up in the flow of his thoughts. It was still quite early in the morning, and he had only slept fitfully, but he had given up trying to sleep. Ever since the realisation he could not get his own film made, he had been unsettled day and night with the thought he might finally have to accept defeat in his mission to the community. He had not guided a single person in Kirknane to the enlightenment he had himself experienced and he felt instinctively that he had now come to the end of finding any way to do so – that there was in fact no realistic way at all in a society as degraded as that of Kirknane's. He was now trying to rationalise his way to the same conclusion.

Suddenly, his thoughts were interrupted by the sound of post being put through his letter box and landing on the hall floor. It was a measure of his preoccupation that he hadn't heard the postman coming before he reached his door. Getting post was not that usual for Stephen, given his lack of engagement with the rest of Kirknane, so curiosity, and the diversion it offered from uncomfortable thoughts, sent him immediately to see what had been delivered. When he got to the hall he could see there was just the one item of post, but larger and thicker than was typical of what mail he got. He immediately picked it up and examined the envelope front and back for any clues as to who had sent it and why. Whatever hope he had of it being anything positive, however, was instantly dispelled when he saw the name of the Community Party on the envelope. It was only then that he remembered the election campaign for the community's government was now underway and commencing as usual with the launch of party manifestos. It would no doubt be won once more by the governing Community Party, he thought, and add further years to their long and continuous rule. Nevertheless, he decided to open the envelope there and then and read its contents, for it would be a welcome distraction from the process of coming to terms with the failure of his mission. When he opened the envelope and took out its contents it was, as he had expected, the manifesto of the Community Party for the coming election. He took it back to his chair at his bedroom window to read it, but discarded the envelope on the way.

Once seated, Stephen began to read his way through the manifesto. As was normally the case, it covered every aspect of the life of the community, for there was no aspect that should not come under the democratic scrutiny and approval of the community of Kirknane. Stephen came to the part of the manifesto covering cultural issues, and which was subtitled: 'A vision for culture.' As he expected, the Community Party acclaimed the launch of its short film scheme. Knowing how flawed it was, Stephen winced at its self-congratulatory praise. Nothing else in the part on culture bothered him any more than usual until, to his surprise, he alighted on a section about the diving pool (sport was treated as culture in Kirknane). His pulse raced a little, for it was his filling of the diving pool - watching entranced at the water rising ever higher and becoming ever deeper, and evoking his experience of the reservoir itself – that, other than his writing, had probably given him the profoundest and most pleasing experience of his life in Kirknane. It was also in regard to the diving pool that he had come the nearest to achieving any success in his mission. It was a degree of shock and horror, however, and nothing at all positive, that Stephen felt as he read what the manifesto said about the diving pool, for it announced the Community Party's intention to end its use for diving, partly on the grounds that an experimental re-opening of the pool had not seen a single person using it, and use it instead as the plunge pool for a new water flume.

Far from reading the Community Party's manifesto as a diversion from acknowledging and coming to terms with the end of his mission, Stephen now saw his mission in a new light. Now he knew it was Kirknane politics that had caused the diving pool to be re-opened and then closed again, and seemingly as part of a cynical justification for converting it to a plunge pool. Certainly, he could not recall any effort of any kind to encourage anyone to use the diving pool during its temporary re-opening. Indeed, he remembered the staff at the Swimming Pool not knowing why he had been instructed to fill it when he asked them about it. John Gattonside had said how earlier use of the diving pool had required a member of staff to act as a dedicated lifeguard because of the pool being cut off from the swimming pool, so if there was any serious intention for people to use the diving pool the staff would therefore have been appropriately directed in that regard and would thus be aware of its intended re-use. He doubted the staff were given any direction or encouragement to get people to use it once it was 'available'.

Stephen could not think of any other use for a water flume than a plunge pool that was more in opposition to the virtues of a diving pool. A plunge pool would do nothing more than safely 'land' the users of a water flume that in itself was nothing more than a wet slide. The users of such a slide would not have the sensibility in which the plunge pool could operate as an abode of the Power, although Stephen could not deny its potential at a more basic level than diving.

It didn't take Stephen long to see not only that a new opposition was created between a 'good' diving pool and a 'bad' diving pool as plunge pool, to match the same oppositions of 'good' and 'bad' versions of the novel *The Fugitive*, the poem *The Reservoir*, the swimming manual, the diving manual, and the film *Poisoned Chalice*, but that implicit in the political dimension to the diving pool opposition was another opposition between a 'good' manifesto and the Community Party's 'bad' manifesto. There would therefore, Stephen thought, be further 'bad' policies, in addition to the short film scheme and the water flume with plunge pool, in other parts of the 'bad' manifesto, that he had either yet to read or had already unconsciously passed over while browsing it, that would also have 'good' versions in opposition.

With his newfound awareness, Stephen carefully re-read those parts of the manifesto he had already covered then read the rest of it. He did indeed come across other 'bad' policies, covering different subjects, that could be categorised as similar in nature and effect to the one about the diving pool, and that he could therefore conceive of as having 'good' versions in opposition. It was only now that he understood the vital role the political system had in the community's malaise and as an instrument of the community's power. He saw it as a kind of toxic irrigation system poisoning the community. However, he also saw that it could be utilised positively to irrigate the community mentally and cure its malaise - just as he had wanted to since discovering the Power.

This made Stephen wonder what the 'good' manifesto might contain; not only in opposition to the 'bad' manifesto but in other ways as well. In anticipation, he took in his hands the jotter and pen he always kept ready on his bedroom window sill for writing things down as they came to him. Then, as he started to contemplate what he might write down as a manifesto, he experienced a strange feeling of calm and tranquility, and an alluring sense of profound possibility - and saw Kirknane's politics as a reservoir in the community and abode of the Power!

From this reservoir Stephen proceeded to draw out the policies he thought were required to create the physical and mental infrastructure – the irrigation system - that would remedy the existing deficiencies of Kirknane and create a new, fully virtuous community.

Once he had sated himself with this lengthy but profoundly satisfying exercise, he stopped and basked a little while in his achievement. However, he soon had to acknowledge that what he had written out could not – would not - happen.

He then had to ask himself what he was to do with his manifesto and his realisation of how much politics was a dynamic in the condition of the community. He knew he could not ignore either if he was in fact to continue with his mission. It would thus, he thought, have to be in some significant way political, and almost certainly include campaigning against the water flume with its plunge pool and in favour of the diving pool. He would therefore make explicit his dissent against the community. Despite all he had been through, however, Stephen believed he had so far managed to disguise his true thoughts and feelings even from those he had interacted with in regard to his mission. He still led a private, anonymous life: a life he treasured considerably despite its defects. If he sacrificed that life through explicit dissent, what might - or would - happen? His politics would be so alien to the community, and so hostile to its values, that he would not only certainly fail, but suffer in some way at the hands of the community - probably severely - for his efforts, and become some kind of martyr, but without anyone to appreciate his martyrdom. In particular, he could lose his job as a water operative, at least through alleged abuse of his position, and therefore the only way he could return to the reservoir.

Thirty

Stephen's arrest and trial was a nightmare...

Stephen was sound asleep, so he didn't hear the common door creak open and shut as the two men entered his tenement. Neither did he hear their steps on the stone floor of the common stair resounding through the building as they made their way up to his flat. What he did hear, what woke him, was his doorbell ringing.

At first he wondered if he had dreamt it, for he seldom had anyone come to his front door and it was too early an hour even for the postman. As if on cue, the doorbell rang again and convinced him he hadn't dreamt it. With a mixture of apprehension and curiosity, he got out of bed and went to his front door to see who was there. Opening the door, he found two smartly dressed men of larger than average build standing side by side and looking at him with a solemn demeanour.

'Mr. Stephen Whyte?' one of them asked in a low, polite-like but commanding tone.

'Yes,' replied Stephen, somewhat hesitantly.

'We are police officers - can we come in?' asked the same man, and in the same tone, indicating they were coming in anyway. At the same time both men displayed their identity cards to Stephen by holding them out to him with outstretched arms. He glanced at both of the cards, for ignoring them, or carefully comparing the photos on them with the two men standing before him, would have been equally inappropriate.

'Yes,' Stephen replied, again somewhat hesitantly, for he was now more apprehensive and curious than he was before. He held the door wide open for the two men to enter. Once they were inside and Stephen had closed the door, the two men lost no time with the purpose of their visit.

'Stephen Whyte, we are arresting you on suspicion of attempting to subvert the community of Kirknane. You must get dressed immediately and come with us.'

Stephen went back to his bedroom to get dressed, accompanied by one of the police officers. As he got dressed, and despite his shock at his arrest, he managed to feel a certain perverse pride at the idea of him being worthy of arrest on suspicion of 'subversion'. It made his conduct seem very important, and even in some way validated - even though he knew the community was subverting itself.

Over the next few days Stephen was interrogated about various aspects of his life of the past few years. He was also informed that his flat was being searched as part of the investigation into his alleged subversive activities. There then followed a period during which the responses he had given to his interrogators, as well as the results of the search of his flat, were examined by the Procurator Fiscal to determine on prosecution. In the meantime, given the seriousness of the pending charge or charges against him, he was kept in custody.

After a few days of awaiting the outcome, and increasingly wanting simply to know what was going to happen regardless of what that was, Stephen was finally informed that he was being put on trial for subversive activities and would remain in custody until the trial took place.

After three months of incarceration - and nervous anticipation - the trial began. Before a panel of three judges and - to Stephen's particular dismay - a jury of Kirknane's citizens, the evidence of his subversive activities was presented by a procession of witnesses for the prosecution. To Stephen, it was a somewhat surreal review of his life over the last year or so viewed through the distorting prism of his prosecution as each witness in turn gave their damning testimony of what he had said and done.

The first witness was Davina Corrie, the commissioning editor at Blackburns the publishers. She testified that Stephen had submitted a novel to her that was set in a barely disguised Kirknane, elitist in style, and depicted as its hero someone rebelling against the community and its values. The prosecutor added his own sneering observation that, as his 'scribblings' had never been good enough for publication, Stephen's claim to be a writer was a vain assertion unvalidated by anyone else in the community.

Then the water operatives Stephen had worked with each spoke of how he had approached them at the water company depot, when they were on their own, and tried to convert them to his weird and deviant beliefs.

This was followed by staff of the swimming pool recounting Stephen's questioning of the instruction given to him to re-activate the diving pool. Although this was not itself evidence of subversion, it contributed to the portrayal of his rebelliousness.

After that, some members of the Swimming Club testified to Stephen's sinister seeming observation of them during a number of club sessions, and included how he sometimes appeared to be making notes about them as he watched them.

Members of the Film Club followed with further testimony of the same kind.

They were followed in turn by John Gattonside who, while carefully avoiding implicating himself, related Stephen's visit to his flat in a way suggesting Stephen's guilt.

Although the testimony of the Swimming Club and Film Club members was not inherently all that damning, the counsel for the prosecution skilfully made it seem more incriminating than it was by tying it in with other, stronger evidence. In the case of John Gattonside, the strong impression was created by the prosecution counsel that Stephen was trying to recruit Gattonside to some conspiracy related to his subversive activities and beliefs.

Then came a member of staff from the library, who described how he had become suspicious of Stephen's visits there and, while observing him, saw him throw something dismissively into a bin while muttering 'Kirknane' followed by something indistinct followed by 'and its nonsense,' and how he had retrieved what Stephen had binned to find it was a government information leaflet.

The most damning evidence of all was provided by the last two witnesses. Firstly, a police officer testified that in the search of Stephen's flat they had found a document - in Stephen's handwriting as confirmed by a handwriting expert - setting out a complete policy programme for turning Kirknane into a reactionary elite tyranny.

Secondly, a psychiatrist testified to the panel of judges and the jury that his psychological assessment of Stephen found him to have a 'narcissistic personality disorder with associated antisocial and delusional tendencies.' (Stephen appreciated the irony of such rare articulacy in Kirknane being used to condemn his own heightened articulation of his own 'diagnosis' of the community). As an example of Stephen's mental state, the psychiatrist related a particular incident during the assessment: Stephen had defiantly and grandly asserted that the programme discovered in the search of his home was in fact his manifesto for the coming elections, and that his intention – indeed his mission, his fate – was to usurp the existing regime and power of the community and to become the single Minister for the entire government of the Community of the Kirknane, or more precisely its Minister for Irrigation. Just as he had ministered the reservoir in the hills for the community, so he would minister the reservoirs in Kirknane itself: reservoirs, he asserted, that took numerous forms both physical and mental, and that people were not yet aware of but needed to be. Furthermore, his ministry would bring a great revelation to the people of Kirknane that would let them see everything in a new light, transforming for the better their lives forever, and thereby sweep away the profound defects of modern day Kirknane. He had also - 'bizarrely' – stated that the charge of subversion should be extended to the entire community as they had subverted Kirknane's regime and the community's power in creating their own reservoirs and abodes of the Power.

The psychiatrist further stated that Stephen's reservoirs were a psychological projection in which the 'Power' in the reservoirs represented the idealisation of his delusional idea of his own power. Indeed, Stephen had himself made the point during his assessment that, like all human beings, he was 70 per cent water.

What the psychiatrist did not relate was that, ever since his arrest, Stephen had become increasingly angry and resentful of what he saw as his unjustified persecution. In particular, the comprehensive and insensitive intrusions into his hitherto very private life: the thorough search of his home, the reading of all his personal papers, and the various interrogations that culminated in his sessions with the psychiatrist. It was these intrusions that finally provoked in Stephen the outburst related by the psychiatrist, but his outburst was as exceptional as the situation he found himself in, and why it escaped any habit or wisdom of non-utterance.

Stephen himself refused to be questioned by the prosecution by asserting his right not to be a witness against himself.

In contrast to the extensive and damning evidence against Stephen provided by the prosecution, his court appointed counsel had not been able to find anyone who would speak in his defence, nor had he been able to conceive a convincing means of refuting the prosecution's case - the evidence was too much against Stephen. He had therefore advised Stephen that the best approach to take was to accept the psychiatrist's assessment of him without equivocation and plead diminished responsibility on mental health grounds, and that such a plea in mitigation offered him the best result he could realistically hope for. He was to expect, however, some sort of incarceration. With Stephen's assent, his counsel made such a plea and abstained from offering any other defence. Stephen knew his counsel was incapable of any effective cross-examination of the prosecution witnesses, and any coherent and eloquent testimony he himself gave would not be properly appreciated by either the jury or the judges. Both efforts, however, might undermine his plea.

With the prosecution's presentation of its case now over, the jury retired to consider their verdict. Whatever the verdict was, Stephen could not see what difference it would make, for he could not imagine a punishment any much different or worse than his current alienation and isolation from the community in the cell he already lived in in the form of his flat. His one potential significant loss was his view from his bedroom window of the countryside and the hills beyond that held the reservoir. He expected it would be replaced by the oppressive, dull light of a cell with a small window: a window not low enough to allow a comfortable view, and a view with little merit in any case - such was the punitive nature of Kirknane's justice.

Thirty One

Stephen opened his eyes and immediately realised that it was much earlier than his normal time for waking up and that he had been sweating profusely - particularly, it seemed, on his face. He looked over to his bedside clock, its face lit up in the dark, and saw that it was only four o'clock; that tallied with the utterly silent and still atmosphere of his bedroom and his flat generally. He knew that to get back to sleep he must first refresh himself or his sweaty state would keep him awake, so he got up and went through to the bathroom. Switching the light on as he entered, he put the plug in the basin and ran the cold water tap. As he waited for the basin to fill, he put his right hand under the tap he had turned on and felt the cold, fresh water as it ran through his fingers. It made him think back to the reservoir, where the water had come from, and how that reservoir and its water was now making a little reservoir in his bathroom basin. As he watched it fill up, it reminded him of how he had watched in wonder at the diving pool fill up - mesmerised by the water slowly rising and becoming ever deeper - as it became another reservoir, another abode of the Power.

Once the basin was full, Stephen turned off the tap and paused for a few seconds to look at the water. When its surface had become completely still, even this little reservoir seemed to have the same beguiling qualities of the reservoirs he had experienced previously. He could even sense the Power a little, although he wasn't sure whether this time, at least, he was simply willing it into existence - perhaps as a small act of defiance (or subversion!). Then he dipped his entire face into the water and held it there for a few seconds before taking it out again. That was better! He dabbed his face with the hand towel that hung on the back of the bathroom door, but deliberately left his face a little damp with the cold water to help remain cool when he went back to bed. He then turned back to the basin to empty it, but as he did so he saw himself in the mirror on the wall above the basin and, without thinking, felt compelled to draw himself up to his reflection to have a close look at himself. His curiosity at how he might find himself reflected in the mirror gave the mirror a sense of possibility, mystery and profundity that he now so easily associated with a reservoir, an abode of the Power. Indeed the mirror was like a screen and the glass had a water-like quality making it seem like the utterly still surface of water he had experienced at the reservoir and after. At first, to Stephen, as he saw himself in the mirror, he looked his usual self, but then he felt - saw perhaps - there was something more. He put his face right up to the mirror to the point of almost touching it and stared at himself staring back at himself. It seemed as if his reflection was another person and not him, and that in the depths of the mirror was someone and something he didn't know - and perhaps didn't want to know. Disturbed by these thoughts, he pulled himself back from the mirror. He took the basin plug out and watched the surface of the water slowly lowered as the water drained away until it - and with it, the reservoir, the swimming pool, and the diving pool - had completely gone. He then switched off the bathroom light, making the mirror - and with it, the screen and other reservoir – disappear, no longer to be seen. In the dark, Stephen made his way back to his bedroom.

The End

The Laverock's Nest Press

29156832R00056

Made in the USA
Charleston, SC
04 May 2014